I0764582

The Power of Darkness and other Chilling Tales

By

Edith Nesbit

Cover Photograph: Ghetu Daniel

ISBN: 978-1-78139-190-7

Contents

The Power of Darkness

by

Edith Nesbit

It was an enthusiastic send-off. Half the students from her atelier were there, and twice as many more from other studios. She had been the belle of the Artists' Quarter in Montparnasse for three golden months. Now she was off to the Riviera to meet her people, and everyone she knew was at the Gare de Lyon to catch the last glimpse of her. And, as had been more than once said late of an evening, "to see her was to love her". She was one of those agitating blondes, with the naturally rippled hair, the rounded rose-leaf cheeks, the large violet-blue eyes, that looked all things and meant Heaven alone knew how little. She held her court like a queen, leaning out of the carriage window and receiving bouquets, books, journals, long last words, and last longing looks. All eyes were on her, and her eyes were for all-and her smile. For all but one, that is. Not a single glance went Edward's way, and Edward-tall, lean, gaunt, with big eyes, straight nose, and the mouth somewhat too small, too beautiful-seemed to grow thinner and paler before one's eyes. One pair of eyes at least saw the miracle worked, the paling of what had seemed absolute pallor, the revelation of the bones of a face that seemed already covered but by the thinnest possible veil of flesh.

And the man whose eyes saw this rejoiced, for he loved her, like the rest, or not like the rest, and he had had Edward's face before him for the last month, in that secret shrine where we set the loved and the hated, the shrine that is lighted by a million lamps kindled at the soul's flame, the shrine that leaps into dazzling glow when the candles are out and one lies alone on hot pillows to outface the night and the light as best one may.

"Oh, goodbye; goodbye, all of you," said Rose. "I shall miss you. Oh, you don't know how I shall miss you all!"

She gathered the eyes of her friends and her worshippers in a glance, as one gathers jewels on a silken string. The eyes of Edward alone seemed to escape her.

"En voiture, messieurs et dames!"

Folk drew back from the train. There was a whistle.

And then at the very last little moment of all, as the train pulled itself together for the start, her eyes met Edward's eyes. And the other man saw the meeting, and he knew-which was more than Edward did.

So when, the light of life having been borne away in the retreating train, the broken-hearted group dispersed, the other man-whose name, by the way, was Vincent-linked his arm in Edward's and asked, cheerily:

"Whither away, sweet nymph?"

"I'm off home," said Edward. "The seven-twenty to Calais."

"Sick of Paris?"

"One has to see one's people sometimes, don't you know, hang it all!" was Edward's way of expressing the longing that tore him for the old house among the brown woods of Kent.

"No attraction here now, eh?"

"The chief attraction has gone, certainly," Edward made himself say.

"But there are as good fish in the sea-"

"Fishing isn't my trade," said Edward.

"The beautiful Rose!" said Vincent.

Edward raised hurriedly the only shield he could find. It happened to be the truth as he saw it.

"Oh," he said, "of course, we're all in love with her-and all hopelessly."

Vincent perceived that this was truth, as Edward saw it. "What are you going to do till your train goes?" he asked.

"I don't know. Café, I suppose, and a vilely early dinner."

"Let's look in at the Musée Grévin," said Vincent.

The two were friends. They had been schoolfellows, and this is a link that survives many a strain too strong to be resisted by more intimate and vital bonds. And they were fellow-students, though that counts for little or much-as you take it. Besides, Vincent knew something about Edward that no one else of their age and standing even guessed. He knew that Edward was afraid of the dark, and why. He had found it out that Christmas which the two had spent at an English country house. The house was full; there was a dance. There were to be theatricals.

Early in the new year the hostess meant to "move house" to an old convent, built in Tudor times, a beautiful palace with terraces and clipped yew trees, castellated battlements, a moat, swans, and a ghost story.

"You boys," she said, "must put up with a shake-down in the new house. I hope the ghost won't worry you. She's an old lady in a figured satin dress. Comes and breathes softly on the back of your neck when you're shaving. Then you see her in the glass, and as often as not you cut your throat." She laughed. So did Edward and Vincent and the other young men. There were seven or eight of them.

But that night, when sparse candles had lighted "the boys" to their rooms, when the last pipe had been smoked, the last "Goodnight" said, there came a fumbling with the handle of Vincent's door. Edward came in, an unwieldy figure, clasping pillows, trailing blankets.

"What the deuce?" queried Vincent, in natural amazement.

"I'll turn in here on the floor if you don't mind," said Edward. "I know it's beastly rot, but I can't stand it. The room they've put me into, it's an attic as big as a barn-and there's a great door at the end, eight feet high, and it leads into a sort of horror hole-bare beams and rafters, and black as night. I know I'm an abject duffer, but there it is-I can't face it."

Vincent was sympathetic; though he had never known a night terror that could not be exorcized by pipe, book, and candle.

"I know, old chap. There's no reasoning about these things," said he, and so on.

"You can't despise me more than I despise myself," Edward said. "I feel a crawling hound. But it is so. I had a scare when I was a kid, and it seems to have left a sort of brand on me. I'm branded "coward", old man, and the feel of it's not nice."

Again Vincent was sympathetic, and the poor little tale came out. How Edward, eight years old, and greedy as became his little years, had sneaked down, night-clad, to pick among the outcomings of a dinner party, and how, in the hall, dark with the light of an "artistic" coloured glass lantern, a white figure had suddenly faced him--leaned towards him, it seemed, pointed lead-white hands at his heart. That next day, finding him weak from his fainting fit, had shown the horror to be but a statue, a new purchase of his father's, had mattered not one whit.

Edward shared Vincent's room, and Vincent, alone of all men, shared Edward's secret.

And now, in Paris, Rose speeding away towards Cannes, Vincent said:

"Let's look in at the Musée Grévin."

The Musée Grévin is a waxwork show. Your mind, at the word, flies instantly to the excellent exhibition founded by the worthy Mme Tussaud. And you think you know what waxworks mean. But you are wrong. The Musée Grévin contains the work of artists for a nation of artists. Wax-modelled and retouched till it seems as near life as death is: this is what one sees at the Musée Grévin.

"Let's look in at the Musée Grévin," said Vincent. He remembered the pleasant thrill the Musée had given him, and wondered what sort of a thrill it would give his friend.

"I hate museums," said Edward.

"This isn't a museum," Vincent said, and truly; "it's just wax-works."

"All right," said Edward, indifferently. And they went.

They reached the doors of the Musée in the grey-brown dusk of a February evening.

One walks along a bare, narrow corridor, much like the entrance to the stalls of the Standard Theatre, and such daylight as there may be fades away behind one, and one finds oneself in a square hall, heavily decorated, and displaying with its electric lights Loie Fuller in her accordion-pleated skirts, and one or two other figures not designed to quicken the pulse.

"It's very like Mme Tussaud's," said Edward.

"Yes," Vincent said; "isn't it?"

Then they passed through an arch, and beheld a long room with waxen groups life-like behind glass-the coulisses of the Opera, Kitchener at Fashoda-this last with a desert background lit by something convincingly like desert sunlight.

"By Jove!" said Edward. "That's jolly good."

"Yes," said Vincent again; "isn't it?"

Edward's interest grew.

The things were so convincing, so very nearly alive. Given the right angle, their glass eyes met one's own, and seemed to exchange with one meaning glances.

Vincent led the way to an arched door labelled "Galerie de la Révolution."

There one saw-almost in the living, suffering body--poor Marie Antoinette in prison in the Temple, her little son on his couch of rags, the rats eating from his platter, the brutal Simon calling to him from the grated window. One almost heard the words: "Holà, little Capet!-are you asleep?"

One saw Marat bleeding in his bath, the brave Charlotte eyeing him; the very tiles of the bathroom, the glass of the windows, with, outside, the very sunlight, as it seemed, of 1793, on that "yellow July evening, the thirteenth of the month."

The spectators did not move in a public place among waxwork figures. They peeped through open doors into rooms where history seemed to be relived. The rooms were lighted each by its own sun or lamp or candle. The spectators walked among shadows that might have oppressed a nervous person.

"Fine, eh?" said Vincent.

"Yes," said Edward; "it's wonderful." A turn of a comer brought them to a room. Marie Antoinette fainting, supported by her ladies; poor, fat Louis by the window looking literally sick.

"What's the matter with them all?" said Edward.

"Look at the window," said Vincent.

There was a window to the room. Outside was sunshine-the sunshine of 1792-and gleaming in it, blonde hair flowing, red mouth half-open, what seemed the just-severed head of a beautiful woman. It was raised on a pike, so that it seemed to be looking in at the window.

"I say," said Edward, and the head on the pike seemed to sway before his eyes.

"Mme de Lamballe. Good thing, isn't it?" said Vincent.

"It's altogether too much of a good thing," said Edward. "Look here-I've had enough of this."

"Oh, you must just see the Catacombs," said Vincent; "nothing gruesome, you know. Only early Christians being married and baptized, and all that."

He led the way down some clumsy steps to the cellars which the genius of a great artist has transformed into the exact semblance of the old Catacombs at Rome. The same rough hewing of rock, the same sacred tokens engraved strongly and simply; and among the arches of these subterranean burrowings the life of the early Christians, their sacraments, their joys, their sorrows-all expressed in groups of waxwork as like life as death is.

"But this is very fine, you know," said Edward, getting his breath again after Mme de Lamballe, and his imagination loved the thought of the noble sufferings and refrainings of these first lovers of the crucified Christ.

"Yes," said Vincent, for the third time; "isn't it?"

They passed the baptism and the burying and the marriage. The tableaux were sufficiently lighted, but little light strayed to the narrow passage where the two men walked, and the darkness seemed to press, tangible as a bodily presence, against Edward's shoulder. He glanced backward.

"Come," he said; "I've had enough."

"Come on, then," said Vincent.

They turned the corner, and a blaze of Italian sunlight struck at their eyes with positive dazzlement. There lay the Coliseum-tier on tier of eager faces under the blue sky of Italy. They were level with the arena. In the arena were crosses; from them drooped bleeding figures. On the sand beasts prowled, bodies lay. They saw it all through bars. They seemed to be in the place where the chosen victims waited their turn, waited for the lions and the crosses, the palm and the crown. Close by Edward was a group-an old man, a woman, and children. He could have touched them with his hand. The woman and the man stared in an agony of terror straight in the eyes of a snarling tiger, ten feet long, that stood up on its hind feet and clawed through the bars at them. The youngest child only, unconscious of the horror, laughed in the very face of it. Roman soldiers, unmoved in military vigilance, guarded the group of martyrs. In a low cage to the left more wild beasts cringed and seemed to growl, unfed. Within the grating, on the wide circle of yellow sand, lions and tigers drank the blood of Christians. Close against the bars a great lion sucked the chest of a corpse, on whose bloodstained face the horror of the death-agony was printed plain.

"Good heavens!" said Edward. Vincent took his arm suddenly, and he started with what was almost a shriek.

"What a nervous chap you are!" said Vincent, complacently, as they regained the street where the lights were, and the sound of voices and the movement of live human beings-all that warms and awakens nerves almost paralysed by the life in death of waxen immobility.

"I don't know," said Edward. "Let's have a vermouth, shall we? There's something uncanny about those wax things. They're like life-but they're much more like death. Suppose they moved? I don't feel at all sure that they don't move, when the lights are all out and there's no one there."

He laughed.

"I suppose you were never frightened, Vincent?"

"Yes, I was once," said Vincent, sipping his absinthe. "Three other men and I were taking turns by twos to watch by a dead man. It was a fancy of his mother's. Our time was up, and the other watch hadn't come. So my chap-the one who was watching with me, I mean-went to fetch them. I didn't think I should mind. But it was just like you say."

"How?"

"Why," I kept thinking, "Suppose it should move. It was so like life. And if it did move, of course it would have been because it was alive, and I ought to have been glad, because the man was my friend. But all the same, if he had moved I should have gone mad."

"Yes," said Edward, "that's just exactly it."

Vincent called for a second absinthe.

"But a dead body's different to waxworks," he said. "I can't understand anyone being frightened of them."

"Oh, can't you?" The contempt in the other's tone stung him. "I bet you wouldn't spend a night alone in that place."

"I bet you five pounds I do!"

"Done," said Edward, briskly. "At least, I would if you'd got five pounds."

"But I have. I'm simply rolling. I've sold my Dejanira; didn't you know? I shall win your money though, anyway. But you couldn't do it, old man. I suppose you'll never outgrow that childish scare."

"You might shut up about that," said Edward, shortly.

"Oh, it's nothing to be ashamed of; some women are afraid of mice or spiders. I say, does Rose know you're a coward?"

"Vincent!"

"No offence, old boy. One may as well call a spade a spade. Of course, you've got tons of moral courage and all that. But you are afraid of the dark-and waxworks!"

"Are you trying to quarrel with me?"

"Heaven in its mercy forbid. But I bet you wouldn't spend a night in the Musée Grévin and keep your senses."

"What's the stake?"

"Anything you like."

"Make it that if I do you'll never speak to Rose again, and, what's more, that you'll never speak to me," said Edward, white-hot, knocking down a chair as he rose.

"Done," said Vincent. "But you'll never do it. Keep your hair on. Besides, you're off home."

"I shall be back in ten days. I'll do it then," said Edward, and was off before the other could answer.

Then Vincent, left alone, sat still, and over his third absinthe remembered how, before she had known Edward, Rose had smiled on him more than the others, he thought. He thought of her wide, lovely eyes, her wild-rose cheeks, the scented curves of her hair, and then and there the devil entered into him.

In ten days Edward would undoubtedly try to win his wager. He would try to spend the night in the Musée Grévin. Perhaps something could be arranged before that. If one knew the place thoroughly! A little scare would serve Edward right for being the man to whom that last glance of Rose's had been given.

Vincent dined lightly, but with conscientious care-and as he dined he thought. Something might be done by tying a string to one of the figures and making it move when Edward was going through that impossible night among the effigies that are so like life-so like death. Something that was not the devil said:

"You may frighten him out of his wits."

And the devil answered: "Nonsense; do him good. He oughtn't to be such a schoolgirl."

Anyway, the five pounds might as well be won tonight as any other night. He would take a greatcoat, sleep sound in the place of horrors, and the people who opened it in the morning to sweep and dust would bear witness that he had passed the night there. He thought he might trust to the French love of a sporting wager to keep him from any bother with the authorities.

So he went in among the crowd, and looked about among the waxworks for a place to hide in. He was not in the least afraid of these lifeless images. He had always been able to control his nervous tremors in his time. He was not even afraid of being frightened, which, by the way, is the worst fear of all.

As one looks at the room of the poor little Dauphin one sees a door to the left. It opens out of the room on to blackness. There were few people in the gallery. Vincent watched, and, in a moment when he was alone, stepped over the barrier and through this door. A narrow passage ran round behind the wall of the room. Here he hid, and when the gallery was deserted he looked out across the body of little Capet to the gaoler at the window. There was a soldier at the window too. Vincent amused himself with the fancy that this soldier might walk round the passage at the back of the room and tap him on the shoulder in the darkness. Only the head and shoulders of the soldier and the gaoler showed, so, of course, they could not walk, even if they were something that was not waxwork.

Presently he himself went along the passage and round to the window where they were. He found that they had legs. They were full-sized figures, dressed completely in the costume of the period.

"Thorough the beggars are, even the parts that don't show-artists, upon my word," said Vincent, and went back to his doorway, thinking of the hidden carving behind the capitals of Gothic cathedrals.

But the idea of the soldier who might come behind him in the dark stuck in his mind. Though still a few visitors strolled through the gallery, the closing hour was near. He supposed it would be quite dark. Then-and now he had allowed himself to be amused by the thought of something that should creep up behind him in the dark-he might possibly be nervous in that passage round which, if waxworks could move, the soldier might have come.

"By Jove!" he said; "one might easily frighten oneself by just fancying things. Suppose there were a back way from Marat's bathroom, and instead of the soldier Marat came out of his bath with his wet towels stained with blood and dabbed them against your neck!"

When next the gallery was deserted he crept out. Not because he was nervous, he told himself, but because one might be, and because the passage was draughty, and he meant to sleep.

He went down the steps into the Catacombs, and here he spoke the truth to himself.

"Hang it all," he said, "I was nervous. That fool Edward must have infected me. Mesmeric influences or something."

"Chuck it and go home," said common sense.

"I'm hanged if I do," said Vincent.

There were a good many people in the Catacombs at the moment. Live people. He sucked confidence from their nearness, and went up and down looking for a hiding place.

Through rock-hewn arches he saw a burial scene-a corpse on a bier surrounded by mourners; a great pillar cut off half the still lying figure. It was all still and unemotional as a Sunday-school oleograph. He waited till no one was near, then slipped quickly through the mourning group and hid behind the pillar. Surprising-heartening, too, to find a plain rush-chair there, doubtless set for the resting of tired officials. He sat down in it, comforted his hand with the commonplace lines of its rungs and back. A shrouded waxen figure just behind him to the left of his pillar worried him a little, but the corpse left him unmoved as itself. A far better place, this, than that draughty passage where the soldier with legs kept intruding on the darkness that is always behind one.

Custodians went along the passages issuing orders. A stillness fell. Then, suddenly, all the lights went out.

"That's all right," said Vincent, and composed himself to sleep. But he seemed to have forgotten what sleep was like. He firmly fixed his thoughts on pleasant things-the sale of his picture, dances with Rose, merry evenings with Edward and the others. But the thoughts rushed by him like motes in sunbeams-he could not hold a single one of them, and presently it seemed that he had thought of every pleasant thing that had ever happened to him, and that now, if he thought at all, he must think of the things one wants most to forget. And there would be time in this long night to think much of many things. But now he found that he could no longer think.

The draped effigy just behind him worried him again. He had been trying, at the back of his mind, behind the other thoughts, to strangle the thought of it. But it was there, very close to him. Suppose it put out its hand, its wax hand, and touched him? But it was of wax. It could not move. No, of course not. But suppose it did?

He laughed aloud, a short, dry laugh, that echoed through the vaults. The cheering effect of laughter has been overestimated perhaps. Anyhow, he did not laugh again.

The silence was intense, but it was a silence thick with rustlings and breathings, and movements that his ear, strained to the uttermost, could just not hear. Suppose, as Edward had said, when all the lights were out these things did move. A corpse was a thing that had moved, given a certain condition-life. What if there were a condition, given which these things could move? What if such conditions were present now? What if all of them-Napoleon, yellow-white from his death sleep; the beasts from the amphitheatre, gore dribbling from their jaws; that soldier with the legs-all were drawing near to him in this full silence? Those death masks of Robespierre and Mirabeau-they might float down through the darkness till they touched his face. That head of Mme de Lamballe on the pike might be thrust at him from behind the pillar. The silence throbbed with sounds that could not quite be heard.

"You fool," he said to himself; "your dinner has disagreed with you with a vengeance. Don't be an ass. The whole lot are only a set of big dolls."

He felt for his matches and lighted a cigarette. The gleam of the match fell on the face of the corpse in front of him. The light was brief, and it seemed, somehow, impossible to look by its light in every corner where one would have wished to look. The match burnt his fingers as it went out. And there were only three more matches in the box.

It was dark again, and the image left on the darkness was that of the corpse in front of him. He thought of his dead friend. When the cigarette was smoked out he thought of him more and more, till it seemed that what lay on the bier was not wax. His hand reached forward and drew back more than once. But at last he made it touch the bier and through the blackness travel up along a lean, rigid arm to the wax face that lay there so still. The touch was not reassuring. Just so, and not otherwise, had his dead friend's face felt, to the last touch of his lips. Cold, firm, waxen. People always said the dead were "waxen". How true that was! He had never thought of it before. He thought of it now.

He sat still-so still that every muscle ached; because if you wish to hear the sounds that infest silence you must be very still indeed. He thought of Edward, and of the string he had meant to tie to one of the figures.

"That wouldn't be needed," he told himself. And his ears ached with listening, listening for the sound that, it seemed, must break at last from that crowded silence.

He never knew how long he sat there. To move, to go up, to batter at the door and clamour to be let out--that one could have done if one had had a lantern or even a full matchbox. But in the dark, not knowing the turnings, to feel one's way among these things that were so like life and yet were not alive-to touch, perhaps, these faces that were not dead and yet felt like death! His heart beat heavily in his throat at the thought.

No; he must sit still till morning. He had been hypnotized into this state, he told himself, by Edward, no doubt; it was not natural to him.

Then, suddenly, the silence was shattered. In the dark something moved, and, after those sounds that the silence teemed with, the noise seemed to him thunder-loud. Yet it was only a very, very little sound, just the rustling of drapery, as though something had turned in its sleep. And there was a sigh-not far off.

Vincent's muscles and tendons tightened like fine-drawn wire. He listened. There was nothing more. Only the silence, the thick silence.

The sound had seemed to come from a part of the vault where long ago, when there was light, he had seen a grave being dug for the body of a young girl martyr.

"I will get up and go out," said Vincent. "I have three matches. I am off my head. I shall really be nervous presently if I don't look out."

He got up and struck a match, refused his eyes the sight of the corpse whose waxen face he had felt in the blackness, and made his way through the crowd of figures. By the match's flicker they seemed to make way for him, to turn their heads to look after him. The match lasted till he got to a turn of the rock-hewn passage. His next match showed him the burial scene. The little, thin body of the martyr, palm in hand, lying on the rock-floor in patient waiting, the grave-digger, the mourners. Some standing, some kneeling, one crouched on the ground.

This was where that sound had come from, that rustle, that sigh. He had thought he was going away from it. Instead he had come straight to the spot where, if anywhere, his nerves might be expected to play him false.

"Bah!" he said, and he said it aloud. "The silly things are only wax. Who's afraid?"

His voice sounded loud in the silence that lives with the wax people.

"They're only wax," he said again, and touched with his foot contemptuously the crouching figure in the mantle.

And, as he touched it, it raised its head and looked vacantly at him, and its eyes were bright and alive. He staggered back against another figure and dropped the match. In the new darkness he heard the crouching figure move towards him. Then the darkness fitted in round him very closely.

"What was it exactly that sent poor Vincent mad-you've never told me?" Rose asked the question. She and Edward were looking out over the pines and tamarisks across the blue Mediterranean. They were very happy, because it was their honeymoon.

He told her about the Musée Grévin and the wager, but he did not state the terms of it.

"But why did he think you would be afraid?"

He told her why.

"And then what happened?"

"Why, I suppose he thought there was no time like the present-for his five pounds, you know-and he hid among the waxworks. And I missed my train, and, I thought, there was no time like the present. In fact, dear, I thought if I waited I should have time to make certain of funking it. So I hid there, too. And I put on my big black capuchon, and sat down right in one of the waxwork groups-they couldn't see me from the gallery where you walk. And after they put the lights out I simply went to sleep. And I woke up-and there was a light, and I heard someone say:

"They're only wax," and it was Vincent. "He thought I was one of the wax people till I looked at him; and I expect he thought I was one of them even then, poor chap. And his match went out, and while I was trying to find my railway reading lamp that I'd got near me he began to scream. And the night-watchman came running. And now he thinks everyone in the asylum is made of wax, and he screams if they come near him. They have to put his food near him while he's asleep. It's horrible. I can't help feeling as if it were my fault somehow."

"Of course it's not," said Rose. "Poor Vincent! Do you know, I never really liked him."

There was a pause. Then she said:

"But how was it you weren't frightened?"

"I was," he said, "horribly frightened. It-it-sounds idiotic, but I was really. And yet I had to go through with it. And then I got among the figures of the people in the Catacombs, the people who died for-for things, don't you know, died in such horrible ways. And there they were, so calm-and believing it was all right. So I thought about what they'd gone through. It sounds awful rot, I know, dear, but I expect I was sleepy. Those wax people, they sort of seemed as if they were alive, and were telling me there wasn't anything to be frightened about. I felt as if I was one of them-and they were all my friends, and they'd wake me if anything went wrong. So I just went to sleep."

"I think I understand," she said. But she didn't.

"And the odd thing is," he went on, "I've never been afraid of the dark since. Perhaps his calling me a coward had something to do with it."

"I don't think so," said she. And she was right. But she would never have understood how, nor why.

THE END

Man-size in Marble

by

Edith Nesbit

Although every word of this story is as true as despair, I do not expect people to believe it. Nowadays a "rational explanation" is required before belief is possible. Let me then, at once, offer the "rational explanation" which finds most favour among those who have heard the tale of my life's tragedy. It is held that we were "under a delusion," Laura and I, on that 31st of October; and that this supposition places the whole matter on a satisfactory and believable basis. The reader can judge, when he, too, has heard my story, how far this is an "explanation," and in what sense it is "rational." There were three who took part in this: Laura and I and another man. The other man still lives, and can speak to the truth of the least credible part of my story.

I never in my life knew what it was to have as much money as I required to supply the most ordinary needs--good colours, books, and cab-fares--and when we were married we knew quite well that we should only be able to live at all by "strict punctuality and attention to business." I used to paint in those days, and Laura used to write, and we felt sure we could keep the pot at least simmering. Living in town was out of the question, so we went to look for a cottage in the country, which should be at once sanitary and picturesque. So rarely do these two qualities meet in one cottage that our search was for some time quite fruitless. We tried advertisements, but most of the desirable rural residences which we did look at proved to be lacking in both essentials, and when a cottage chanced to have drains it always had stucco as well and was shaped like a tea-caddy. And if we found a vine or rose-covered porch, corruption invariably lurked within. Our minds got so befogged by the eloquence of house-agents and the rival disadvantages of the fever-traps and outrages to beauty which we had seen and scorned, that I very much doubt whether either of us, on our wedding morning, knew the difference between a house and a haystack. But when we got away from friends and house-agents, on our honeymoon, our wits grew clear again, and we knew a pretty cottage when at last we saw one. It was at Brenzett--a little village set on a hill over against the southern marshes. We had gone there, from the seaside village where we were staying, to see the church, and two fields from the church we found this cottage. It stood quite by itself, about two miles from the village. It was a long, low building, with rooms sticking out in unexpected places. There was a bit of stone-work--ivy-covered and moss-grown, just two old rooms, all that was left of a big house that had once stood there--and round this stone-work the house had grown up. Stripped of its roses and jasmine it would have been hideous. As it stood it was charming, and after a brief examination we took it. It was absurdly cheap. The rest of our honeymoon we spent in grubbing about in second-hand shops in the county town, picking up bits of old oak and Chippendale chairs for our furnishing. We wound up with a run up to town and a visit to Liberty's, and soon the low oak-beamed lattice-windowed rooms began to be home. There was a jolly old-fashioned garden, with grass paths, and no end of hollyhocks and sunflowers, and big lilies. From the window you could see the marsh-pastures, and beyond them the blue, thin line of the sea. We were as happy as the summer was glorious, and settled down into work sooner than we ourselves expected. I was never tired of sketching the view and the wonderful cloud effects from the open lattice, and Laura would sit at the table and write verses about them, in which I mostly played the part of foreground.

We got a tall old peasant woman to do for us. Her face and figure were good, though her cooking was of the homeliest; but she understood all about gardening, and told us all the old names of the coppices and cornfields, and the stories of the smugglers and highwaymen, and, better still, of the "things that walked," and of the "sights" which met one in lonely glens of a starlight night. She was a great comfort to us, because Laura hated housekeeping as much as I loved folklore, and we soon came to leave all the domestic business to Mrs. Dorman, and to use her legends in little magazine stories which brought in the jingling guinea.

We had three months of married happiness, and did not have a single quarrel. One October evening I had been down to smoke a pipe with the doctor--our only neighbour--a pleasant young Irishman. Laura had stayed at home to finish a comic sketch of a village episode for the Monthly Marplot. I left her laughing over her own jokes, and came in to find her a crumpled heap of pale muslin weeping on the window seat.

"Good heavens, my darling, what's the matter?" I cried, taking her in my arms. She leaned her little dark head against my shoulder and went on crying. I had never seen her cry before--we had always been so happy, you see--and I felt sure some frightful misfortune had happened.

"What is the matter? Do speak."

"It's Mrs. Dorman," she sobbed.

"What has she done?" I inquired, immensely relieved.

"She says she must go before the end of the month, and she says her niece is ill; she's gone down to see her now, but I don't believe that's the reason, because her niece is always ill. I believe someone has been setting her against us. Her manner was so queer---"

"Never mind, Pussy," I said; "whatever you do, don't cry, or I shall have to cry too, to keep you in countenance, and then you'll never respect your man again!"

She dried her eyes obediently on my handkerchief, and even smiled faintly.

"But you see," she went on, "it is really serious, because these village people are so sheepy, and if one won't do a thing you may be quite sure none of the others will. And I shall have to cook the dinners, and wash up the hateful greasy plates; and you'll have to carry cans of water about, and clean the boots and knives--and we shall never have any time for work, or earn any money, or anything. We shall have to work all day, and only be able to rest when we are waiting for the kettle to boil!"

I represented to her that even if we had to perform these duties, the day would still present some margin for other toils and recreations. But she refused to see the matter in any but the greyest light. She was very unreasonable, my Laura, but I could not have loved her any more if she had been as reasonable as Whately.

"I'll speak to Mrs. Dorman when she comes back, and see if I can't come to terms with her," I said. "Perhaps she wants a rise in her screw. It will be all right. Let's walk up to the church."

The church was a large and lonely one, and we loved to go there, especially upon bright nights. The path skirted a wood, cut through it once, and ran along the crest of the hill through two meadows, and round the churchyard wall, over which the old yews loomed in black masses of shadow. This path, which was partly paved, was called "the bier-balk," for it had long been the way by which the corpses had been carried to burial. The churchyard was richly treed, and was shaded by great elms which stood just outside and stretched their majestic arms in benediction over the happy dead. A large, low porch let one into the building by a Norman doorway and a heavy oak door studded with iron. Inside, the arches rose into darkness, and between them the reticulated windows, which stood out white in the moonlight. In the chancel, the windows were of rich glass, which showed in faint light their noble colouring, and made the black oak of the choir pews hardly more solid than the shadows. But on each side of the altar lay a grey marble figure of a knight in full plate armour lying upon a low slab, with hands held up in everlasting prayer, and these figures, oddly enough, were always to be seen if there was any glimmer of light in the church. Their names were lost, but the peasants told of them that they had been fierce and wicked men, marauders by land and sea, who had been the scourge of their time, and had been guilty of deeds so foul that the house they had lived in--the big house, by the way, that had stood on the site of our cottage--had been stricken by lightning and the vengeance of Heaven. But for all that, the gold of their heirs had bought them a place in the church. Looking at the bad hard faces reproduced in the marble, this story was easily believed.

The church looked at its best and weirdest on that night, for the shadows of the yew trees fell through the windows upon the floor of the nave and touched the pillars with tattered shade. We sat down together without speaking, and watched the solemn beauty of the old church, with some of that awe which inspired its early builders. We walked to the chancel and looked at the sleeping warriors. Then we rested some time on the stone seat in the porch, looking out over the stretch of quiet moonlit meadows, feeling in every fibre of our being the peace of the night and of our happy love; and came away at last with a sense that even scrubbing and blackleading were but small troubles at their worst.

Mrs. Dorman had come back from the village, and I at once invited her to a tête-à-tête.

"Now, Mrs. Dorman," I said, when I had got her into my painting room, "what's all this about you're not staying with us?"

"I should be glad to get away, sir, before the end of the month," she answered, with her usual placid dignity.

"Have you any fault to find, Mrs. Dorman?"

"None at all, sir; you and your lady have always been most kind, I'm sure---"

"Well, what is it? Are your wages not high enough?"

"No, sir, I gets quite enough."

"Then why not stay?"

"I'd rather not"--with some hesitation--"my niece is ill."

"But your niece has been ill ever since we came."

No answer. There was a long and awkward silence. I broke it.

"Can't you stay for another month?" I asked.

"No, sir. I'm bound to go by Thursday."

And this was Monday!

"Well, I must say, I think you might have let us know before. There's no time now to get any one else, and your mistress is not fit to do heavy housework. Can't you stay till next week?"

"I might be able to come back next week."

I was now convinced that all she wanted was a brief holiday, which we should have been willing enough to let her have, as soon as we could get a substitute.

"But why must you go this week?" I persisted. "Come, out with it."

Mrs. Dorman drew the little shawl, which she always wore, tightly across her bosom, as though she were cold. Then she said, with a sort of effort---

"They say, sir, as this was a big house in Catholic times, and there was a many deeds done here."

The nature of the "deeds" might be vaguely inferred from the inflection of Mrs. Dorman's voice--which was enough to make one's blood run cold. I was glad that Laura was not in the room. She was always nervous, as highly-strung natures are, and I felt that these tales about our house, told by this old peasant woman, with her impressive manner and contagious credulity, might have made our home less dear to my wife.

"Tell me all about it, Mrs. Dorman," I said; "you needn't mind about telling me. I'm not like the young people who make fun of such things."

Which was partly true.

"Well, sir"--she sank her voice--"you may have seen in the church, beside the altar, two shapes."

"You mean the effigies of the knights in armour," I said cheerfully.

"I mean them two bodies, drawed out man-size in marble," she returned, and I had to admit that her description was a thousand times more graphic than mine, to say nothing of a certain weird force and uncanniness about the phrase "drawed out man-size in marble."

"They do say, as on All Saints' Eve them two bodies sits up on their slabs, and gets off of them, and then walks down the aisle, in their marble"--(another good phrase, Mrs. Dorman)--"and as the church clock strikes eleven they walks out of the church door, and over the graves, and along the bier-balk, and if it's a wet night there's the marks of their feet in the morning."

"And where do they go?" I asked, rather fascinated.

"They comes back here to their home, sir, and if any one meets them---"

"Well, what then?" I asked.

But no--not another word could I get from her, save that her niece was ill and she must go. After what I had heard I scorned to discuss the niece, and tried to get from Mrs. Dorman more details of the legend. I could get nothing but warnings.

"Whatever you do, sir, lock the door early on All Saints' Eve, and make the cross-sign over the doorstep and on the windows."

"But has any one ever seen these things?" I persisted.

"That's not for me to say. I know what I know, sir."

"Well, who was here last year?"

"No one, sir; the lady as owned the house only stayed here in summer, and she always went to London a full month afore the night. And I'm sorry to inconvenience you and your lady, but my niece is ill and I must go on Thursday."

I could have shaken her for her absurd reiteration of that obvious fiction, after she had told me her real reasons.

She was determined to go, nor could our united entreaties move her in the least.

I did not tell Laura the legend of the shapes that "walked in their marble," partly because a legend concerning our house might perhaps trouble my wife, and partly, I think, from some more occult reason. This was not quite the same to me as any other story, and I did not want to talk about it till the day was over. I had very soon ceased to think of the legend, however. I was painting a portrait of Laura, against the lattice window, and I could not think of much else. I had got a splendid background of yellow and grey sunset, and was working away with enthusiasm at her lace. On Thursday Mrs. Dorman went. She relented, at parting, so far as to say---

"Don't you put yourself about too much, ma'am, and if there's any little thing I can do next week, I'm sure I shan't mind."

From which I inferred that she wished to come back to us after Hallowe'en. Up to the last she adhered to the fiction of the niece with touching fidelity.

Thursday passed off pretty well. Laura showed marked ability in the matter of steak and potatoes, and I confess that my knives, and the plates, which I insisted upon washing, were better done than I had dared to expect.

Friday came. It is about what happened on that Friday that this is written. I wonder if I should have believed it, if any one had told it to me. I will write the story of it as quickly and plainly as I can. Everything that happened on that day is burnt into my brain. I shall not forget anything, nor leave anything out.

I got up early, I remember, and lighted the kitchen fire, and had just achieved a smoky success, when my little wife came running down, as sunny and sweet as the clear October morning itself. We prepared breakfast together, and found it very good fun. The housework was soon done, and when brushes and brooms and pails were quiet again, the house was still indeed. It is wonderful what a difference one makes in a house. We really missed Mrs. Dorman, quite apart from considerations concerning pots and pans. We spent the day in dusting our books and putting them straight, and dined gaily on cold steak and coffee. Laura was, if possible, brighter and gayer and sweeter than usual, and I began to think that a little domestic toil was really good for her. We had never been so merry since we were married, and the walk we had that afternoon was, I think, the happiest time of all my life. When we had watched the deep scarlet clouds slowly pale into leaden grey against a pale-green sky, and saw the white mists curl up along the hedgerows in the distant marsh, we came back to the house, silently, hand in hand.

"You are sad, my darling," I said, half-jestingly, as we sat down together in our little parlour. I expected a disclaimer, for my own silence had been the silence of complete happiness. To my surprise she said---

"Yes. I think I am sad, or rather I am uneasy. I don't think I'm very well. I have shivered three or four times since we came in, and it is not cold, is it?"

"No," I said, and hoped it was not a chill caught from the treacherous mists that roll up from the marshes in the dying light. No--she said, she did not think so. Then, after a silence, she spoke suddenly---

"Do you ever have presentiments of evil?"

"No," I said, smiling, "and I shouldn't believe in them if I had."

"I do," she went on; "the night my father died I knew it, though he was right away in the north of Scotland." I did not answer in words.

She sat looking at the fire for some time in silence, gently stroking my hand. At last she sprang up, came behind me, and, drawing my head back, kissed me.

"There, it's over now," she said. "What a baby I am! Come, light the candles, and we'll have some of these new Rubinstein duets."

And we spent a happy hour or two at the piano.

At about half-past ten I began to long for the good-night pipe, but Laura looked so white that I felt it would be brutal of me to fill our sitting-room with the fumes of strong cavendish.

"I'll take my pipe outside," I said.

"Let me come, too."

"No, sweetheart, not to-night; you're much too tired. I shan't be long. Get to bed, or I shall have an invalid to nurse to-morrow as well as the boots to clean."

I kissed her and was turning to go, when she flung her arms round my neck, and held me as if she would never let me go again. I stroked her hair.

"Come, Pussy, you're over-tired. The housework has been too much for you."

She loosened her clasp a little and drew a deep breath.

"No. We've been very happy to-day, Jack, haven't we? Don't stay out too long."

"I won't, my dearie."

I strolled out of the front door, leaving it unlatched. What a night it was! The jagged masses of heavy dark cloud were rolling at intervals from horizon to horizon, and thin white wreaths covered the stars. Through all the rush of the cloud river, the moon swam, breasting the waves and disappearing again in the darkness. When now and again her light reached the woodlands they seemed to be slowly and noiselessly waving in time to the swing of the clouds above them. There was a strange grey light over all the earth; the fields had that shadowy bloom over them which only comes from the marriage of dew and moonshine, or frost and starlight.

I walked up and down, drinking in the beauty of the quiet earth and the changing sky. The night was absolutely silent. Nothing seemed to be abroad. There was no skurrying of rabbits, or twitter of the half-asleep birds. And though the clouds went sailing across the sky, the wind that drove them never came low enough to rustle the dead leaves in the woodland paths. Across the meadows I could see the church tower standing out black and grey against the sky. I walked there thinking over our three months of happiness--and of my wife, her dear eyes, her loving ways. Oh, my little girl! my own little girl; what a vision came then of a long, glad life for you and me together!

I heard a bell-beat from the church. Eleven already! I turned to go in, but the night held me. I could not go back into our little warm rooms yet. I would go up to the church. I felt vaguely that it would be good to carry my love and thankfulness to the sanctuary whither so many loads of sorrow and gladness had been borne by the men and women of the dead years.

I looked in at the low window as I went by. Laura was half lying on her chair in front of the fire. I could not see her face, only her little head showed dark against the pale blue wall. She was quite still. Asleep, no doubt. My heart reached out to her, as I went on. There must be a God, I thought, and a God who was good. How otherwise could anything so sweet and dear as she have ever been imagined?

I walked slowly along the edge of the wood. A sound broke the stillness of the night, it was a rustling in the wood. I stopped and listened. The sound stopped too. I went on, and now distinctly heard another step than mine answer mine like an echo. It was a poacher or a wood-stealer, most likely, for these were not unknown in our Arcadian neighbourhood. But whoever it was, he was a fool not to step more lightly. I turned into the wood, and now the footstep seemed to come from the path I had just left. It must be an echo, I thought. The wood looked perfect in the moonlight. The large dying ferns and the brushwood showed where through thinning foliage the pale light came down. The tree trunks stood up like Gothic columns all around me. They reminded me of the church, and I turned into the bier-balk, and passed through the corpse-gate between the graves to the low porch. I paused for a moment on the stone seat where Laura and I had watched the fading landscape. Then I noticed that the door of the church was open, and I blamed myself for having left it unlatched the other night. We were the only people who ever cared to come to the church except on Sundays, and I was vexed to think that through our carelessness the damp autumn airs had had a chance of getting in and injuring the old fabric. I went in. It will seem strange, perhaps, that I should have gone half-way up the aisle before I remembered--with a sudden chill, followed by as sudden a rush of self-contempt--that this was the very day and hour when, according to tradition, the "shapes drawed out man-size in marble" began to walk.

Having thus remembered the legend, and remembered it with a shiver, of which I was ashamed, I could not do otherwise than walk up towards the altar, just to look at the figures--as I said to myself; really what I wanted was to assure myself, first, that I did not believe the legend, and, secondly, that it was not true. I was rather glad that I had come. I thought now I could tell Mrs. Dorman how vain her fancies were, and how peacefully the marble figures slept on through the ghastly hour. With my hands in my pockets I passed up the aisle. In the grey dim light the eastern end of the church looked larger than usual, and the arches above the two tombs looked larger too. The moon came out and showed me the reason. I stopped short, my heart gave a leap that nearly choked me, and then sank sickeningly.

The "bodies drawed out man-size" were gone, and their marble slabs lay wide and bare in the vague moonlight that slanted through the east window.

Were they really gone? or was I mad? Clenching my nerves, I stooped and passed my hand over the smooth slabs, and felt their flat unbroken surface. Had some one taken the things away? Was it some vile practical joke? I would make sure, anyway. In an instant I had made a torch of a newspaper, which happened to be in my pocket, and lighting it held it high above my head. Its yellow glare illumined the dark arches and those slabs. The figures were gone. And I was alone in the church; or was I alone?

And then a horror seized me, a horror indefinable and indescribable--an overwhelming certainty of supreme and accomplished calamity. I flung down the torch and tore along the aisle and out through the porch, biting my lips as I ran to keep myself from shrieking aloud. Oh, was I mad--or what was this that possessed me? I leaped the churchyard wall and took the straight cut across the fields, led by the light from our windows. Just as I got over the first stile, a dark figure seemed to spring out of the ground. Mad still with that certainty of misfortune, I made for the thing that stood in my path, shouting, "Get out of the way, can't you!"

But my push met with a more vigorous resistance than I had expected. My arms were caught just above the elbow and held as in a vice, and the raw-boned Irish doctor actually shook me.

"Would ye?" he cried, in his own unmistakable accents--"would ye, then?"

"Let me go, you fool," I gasped. "The marble figures have gone from the church; I tell you they've gone."

He broke into a ringing laugh. "I'll have to give ye a draught to-morrow, I see. Ye've bin smoking too much and listening to old wives' tales."

"I tell you, I've seen the bare slabs."

"Well, come back with me. I'm going up to old Palmer's--his daughter's ill; we'll look in at the church and let me see the bare slabs."

"You go, if you like," I said, a little less frantic for his laughter; "I'm going home to my wife."

"Rubbish, man," said he; "d'ye think I'll permit of that? Are ye to go saying all yer life that ye've seen solid marble endowed with vitality, and me to go all me life saying ye were a coward? No, sir--ye shan't dout."

The night air--a human voice--and I think also the physical contact with this six feet of solid common sense, brought me back a little to my ordinary self, and the word "coward" was a mental shower-bath.

"Come on, then," I said sullenly; "perhaps you're right."

He still held my arm tightly. We got over the stile and back to the church. All was still as death. The place smelt very damp and earthy. We walked up the aisle. I am not ashamed to confess that I shut my eyes: I knew the figures would not be there. I heard Kelly strike a match.

"Here they are, ye see, right enough; ye've been dreaming or drinking, asking yer pardon for the imputation."

I opened my eyes. By Kelly's expiring vesta I saw two shapes lying "in their marble" on their slabs. I drew a deep breath, and caught his hand.

"I'm awfully indebted to you," I said. "It must have been some trick of light, or I have been working rather hard, perhaps that's it. Do you know, I was quite convinced they were gone."

"I'm aware of that," he answered rather grimly; "ye'll have to be careful of that brain of yours, my friend, I assure ye."

He was leaning over and looking at the right-hand figure, whose stony face was the most villainous and deadly in expression.

"By Jove," he said, "something has been afoot here--this hand is broken."

And so it was. I was certain that it had been perfect the last time Laura and I had been there.

"Perhaps some one has tried to remove them," said the young doctor.

"That won't account for my impression," I objected.

"Too much painting and tobacco will account for that, well enough."

"Come along," I said, "or my wife will be getting anxious. You'll come in and have a drop of whisky and drink confusion to ghosts and better sense to me."

"I ought to go up to Palmer's, but it's so late now I'd best leave it till the morning," he replied. "I was kept late at the Union, and I've had to see a lot of people since. All right, I'll come back with ye."

I think he fancied I needed him more than did Palmer's girl, so, discussing how such an illusion could have been possible, and deducing from this experience large generalities concerning ghostly apparitions, we walked up to our cottage. We saw, as we walked up the garden-path, that bright light streamed out of the front door, and presently saw that the parlour door was open too. Had she gone out?

"Come in," I said, and Dr. Kelly followed me into the parlour. It was all ablaze with candles, not only the wax ones, but at least a dozen guttering, glaring tallow dips, stuck in vases and ornaments in unlikely places. Light, I knew, was Laura's remedy for nervousness. Poor child! Why had I left her? Brute that I was.

We glanced round the room, and at first we did not see her. The window was open, and the draught set all the candles flaring one way. Her chair was empty and her handkerchief and book lay on the floor. I turned to the window. There, in the recess of the window, I saw her. Oh, my child, my love, had she gone to that window to watch for me? And what had come into the room behind her? To what had she turned with that look of frantic fear and horror? Oh, my little one, had she thought that it was I whose step she heard, and turned to meet--what?

She had fallen back across a table in the window, and her body lay half on it and half on the window-seat, and her head hung down over the table, the brown hair loosened and fallen to the carpet. Her lips were drawn back, and her eyes wide, wide open. They saw nothing now. What had they seen last?

The doctor moved towards her, but I pushed him aside and sprang to her; caught her in my arms and cried---

"It's all right, Laura! I've got you safe, wifie."

She fell into my arms in a heap. I clasped her and kissed her, and called her by all her pet names, but I think I knew all the time that she was dead. Her hands were tightly clenched. In one of them she held something fast. When I was quite sure that she was dead, and that nothing mattered at all any more, I let him open her hand to see what she held.

It was a grey marble finger.

THE END

John Charrington's Wedding

by

Edith Nesbit

No one ever thought that May Forster would marry John Charrington; but he thought differently, and things which John Charrington intended had a queer way of coming to pass. He asked her to marry him before he went up to Oxford. She laughed and refused him. He asked her again next time he came home. Again she laughed, tossed her dainty blonde head and again refused. A third time he asked her; she said it was becoming a confirmed bad habit, and laughed at him more than ever.

John was not the only man who wanted to marry her: she was the belle of our village coterie, and we were all in love with her more or less; it was a sort of fashion, like heliotrope ties or Inverness capes. Therefore we were as much annoyed as surprised when John Charrington walked into our little local Club--we held it in a loft over the saddler's, I remember--and invited us all to his wedding.

'Your wedding?'

'You don't mean it?'

'Who's the happy pair? When's it to be?'

John Charrington filled his pipe and lighted it before he replied. Then he said:

'I'm sorry to deprive you fellows of your only joke--but Miss Forster and I are to be married in September.'

'You don't mean it?'

'He's got the mitten again, and it's turned his head.'

'No,' I said, rising, 'I see it's true. Lend me a pistol someone--or a first-class fare to the other end of Nowhere. Charrington has bewitched the only pretty girl in our twenty-mile radius. Was it mesmerism, or a love-potion, Jack?'

'Neither, sir, but a gift you'll never have--perseverance--and the best luck a man ever had in this world.'

There was something in his voice that silenced me, and all chaff of the other fellows failed to draw him further.

The queer thing about it was that when we congratulated Miss Forster, she blushed and smiled and dimpled, for all the world as though she were in love with him, and had been in love with him all the time. Upon my word, I think she had. Women are strange creatures.

We were all asked to the wedding. In Brixham everyone who was anybody knew everybody else who was anyone. My sisters were, I truly believe, more interested in the trousseau than the bride herself, and I was to be best man. The coming marriage was much canvassed at afternoon tea-tables, and at our little Club over the saddler's, and the question was always asked, 'Does she care for him?'

I used to ask that question myself in the early days of their engagement, but after a certain evening in August I never asked it again. I was coming home from the Club through the churchyard. Our church is on a thyme-grown hill, and the turf about it is so thick and soft that one's footsteps are noiseless.

I made no sound as I vaulted the low lichened wall, and threaded my way between the tombstones. It was at the same instant that I heard John Charrington's voice, and saw her. May was sitting on a low flat gravestone, her face turned towards the full splendour of the western sun. Its expression ended, at once and for ever, any question of love for him; it was transfigured to a beauty I should not have believed possible, even to that beautiful little face.

John lay at her feet, and it was his voice that broke the stillness of the golden August evening.

'My dear, my dear, I believe I should come back from the dead if you wanted me!'

I coughed at once to indicate my presence, and passed on into the shadow fully enlightened.

The wedding was to be early in September. Two days before I had to run up to town on business. The train was late, of course, for we are on the South-Eastern, and as I stood grumbling with my watch in my hand, whom should I see but John Charrington and May Forster. They were walking up and down the unfrequented end of the platform, arm in arm, looking into each other's eyes, careless of the sympathetic interest of the porters.

Of course I knew better than to hesitate a moment before burying myself in the booking--office, and it was not till the train drew up at the platform, that I obtrusively passed the pair with my Gladstone, and took the corner in a first-class smoking-carriage. I did this with as good an air of not seeing them as I could assume. I pride myself on my discretion, but if John were travelling alone I wanted his company. I had it.

'Hullo, old man,' came his cheery voice as he swung his bag into my carriage; 'here's luck; I was expecting a dull journey!'

'Where are you off to?' I asked, discretion still bidding me turn my eyes away, though I saw, without looking, that hers were red-rimmed.

'To old Branbridge's,' he answered, shutting the door and leaning out for a last word with his sweetheart.

'Oh, I wish you wouldn't go, John,' she was saying in a low, earnest voice. 'I feel certain something will happen.'

'Do you think I should let anything happen to keep me, and the day after tomorrow our wedding day?'

'Don't go,' she answered, with a pleading intensity which would have sent my Gladstone onto the platform and me after it. But she wasn't speaking to me. John Charrington was made differently: he rarely changed his opinions, never his resolutions.

He only stroked the little ungloved hands that lay on the carriage door.

'I must, May. The old boy's been awfully good to me, and now he's dying I must go and see him, but I shall come home in time for---' the rest of the parting was lost in a whisper and in the rattling lurch of the starting train.

'You're sure to come?' she spoke as the train moved.

'Nothing shall keep me,' he answered; and we steamed out. After he had seen the last of the little figure on the platform he leaned back in his corner and kept silence for a minute.

When he spoke it was to explain to me that his godfather, whose heir he was, lay dying at Peasmarsh Place, some fifty miles away, and had sent for John, and John had felt bound to go.

'I shall be surely back tomorrow,' he said, 'or, if not, the day after, in heaps of time. Thank heaven, one hasn't to get up in the middle of the night to get married nowadays!'

'And suppose Mr Branbridge dies?'

'Alive or dead I mean to be married on Thursday!' John answered, lighting a cigar and unfolding The Times.

At Peasmarsh station we said 'goodbye', and he got out, and I saw him ride off; I went on to London, where I stayed the night.

When I got home the next afternoon, a very wet one, by the way, my sister greeted me with:

'Where's Mr Charrington?'

'Goodness knows,' I answered testily. Every man, since Cain, has resented that kind of question.

'I thought you might have heard from him,' she went on, 'as you're to give him away tomorrow.'

'Isn't he back?' I asked, for I had confidently expected to find him at home.

'No, Geoffrey,' my sister Fanny always had a way of jumping to conclusions, especially such conclusions as were least favourable to her fellow-creatures--'he has not returned, and, what is more, you may depend upon it he won't. You mark my words, there'll be no wedding tomorrow.'

My sister Fanny has a power of annoying me which no other human being possesses.

'You mark my words,' I retorted with asperity, 'you had better give up making such a thundering idiot of yourself. There'll be more wedding tomorrow than ever you'll take the first part in.' A prophecy which, by the way, came true.

But though I could snarl confidently to my sister, I did not feel so comfortable when late that night, I, standing on the doorstep of John's house, heard that he had not returned. I went home gloomily through the rain. Next morning brought a brilliant blue sky, gold sun, and all such softness of air and beauty of cloud as go to make up a perfect day. I woke with a vague feeling of having gone to bed anxious, and of being rather averse to facing that anxiety in the light of full wakefulness.

But with my shaving-water came a note from John which relieved my mind and sent me up to the Forsters with a light heart.

May was in the garden. I saw her blue gown through the hollyhocks as the lodge gates swung to behind me. So I did not go up to the house, but turned aside down the turfed path.

'He's written to you too,' she said, without preliminary greeting, when I reached her side.

'Yes, I'm to meet him at the station at three, and come straight on to the church.'

Her face looked pale, but there was a brightness in her eyes, and a tender quiver about the mouth that spoke of renewed happiness.

'Mr Branbridge begged him so to stay another night that he had not the heart to refuse,' she went on. 'He is so kind, but I wish he hadn't stayed.'

I was at the station at half past two. I felt rather annoyed with John. It seemed a sort of slight to the beautiful girl who loved him, that he should come as it were out of breath, and with the dust of travel upon him, to take her hand, which some of us would have given the best years of our lives to take.

But when the three' o'clock train glided in, and glided out again having brought no passengers to our little station, I was more than annoyed. There was no other train for thirty-five minutes; I calculated that, with much hurry, we might just get to the church in time for the ceremony; but, oh, what a fool to miss that first train! What other man could have done it?

That thirty-five minutes seemed a year, as I wandered round the station reading the advertisements and the timetables, and the company's bye-laws, and getting more and more angry with John Charrington. This confidence in his own power of getting everything he wanted the minute he wanted it was leading him too far. I hate waiting. Everyone does, but I believe I hate it more than anyone else. The three thirty-five was late, of course.

'Drive to the church!' I said, as someone shut the door. 'Mr Charrington hasn't come by this train.'

I ground my pipe between my teeth and stamped with impatience as I watched the signals. Click. The signal went down. Five minutes later I flung myself into the carriage that I had brought for John.

Anxiety now replaced anger. What had become of the man? Could he have been taken suddenly ill? I had never known him have a day's illness in his life. And even so he might have telegraphed. Some awful accident must have happened to him. The thought that he had played her false never--no, not for a moment--entered my head. Yes, some thing terrible had happened to him, and on me lay the task of telling his bride. I almost wished the carriage would upset and break my head so that someone else might tell her, not I, who--but that's nothing to do with this story.

It was five minutes to four as we drew up at the churchyard gate. A double row of eager onlookers lined the path from lychgate to porch. I sprang from the carriage and passed up between them. Our gardener had a good front place near the door. I stopped.

'Are they waiting still, Byles?' I asked, simply to gain time, for of course I knew they were by the waiting crowd's attentive attitude.

'Waiting, sir? No, no, sir; why, it must be over by now.'

'Over! Then Mr Charrington's come?'

To the minute, sir; must have missed you somehow, and I say, sir,' lowering his voice, 'I never see Mr John the least bit so afore, but my opinion is he's been drinking pretty free. His clothes was all dusty and his face like a sheet. I tell you I didn't like the looks of him at all, and the folks inside are saying all sorts of things. You'll see, something's gone very wrong with Mr John, and he's tried liquor. He looked like a ghost, and in he went with his eyes straight before him, with never a look or a word for none of us: him that was always such a gentleman!'

I had never heard Byles make so long a speech. The crowd in the churchyard were talking in whispers and getting ready rice and slippers to throw at the bride and bridegroom. The ringers were ready with their hands on the ropes to ring out the merry peal as the bride and bride-groom should come out.

A murmur from the church announced them; out they came. Byles was right. John Charrington did not look himself. There was dust on his coat, his hair was disarranged. He seemed to have been in some row, for there was a black mark above his eyebrow. He was deathly pale. But his pallor was not greater than that of the bride, who might have been carved in ivory--dress, veil, orange blossoms, face and all.

As they passed out the ringers stooped--there were six of them--and then, on the ears expecting the gay wedding peal, came the slow tolling of the passing bell.

A thrill of horror at so foolish a jest from the ringers passed through us all. But the ringers themselves dropped the ropes and fled like rabbits out into the sunlight. The bride shuddered, and grey shadows came about her mouth, but the bridegroom led her on down the path where the people stood with the handfuls of rice; but the handfuls were never thrown, and the wedding bells never rang. In vain the ringers were urged to remedy their mistake: they protested with many whispered expletives that they would see themselves further first.

In a hush like the hush in the chamber of death the bridal pair passed into their carriage and its door slammed behind them.

Then the tongues were loosed. A babel of anger, wonder, conjecture from the guests and the spectators.

'If I'd seen his condition, sir,' said old Forster to me as we drove off, 'I would have stretched him on the floor of the church, sir, by heaven I would, before I'd have let him marry my daughter!'

Then he put his head out of the window.

'Drive like hell,' he cried to the coachman; 'don't spare the horses.'

He was obeyed. We passed the bride's carriage. I forbore to look at it, and old Forster turned his head away and swore. We reached home before it.

We stood in the doorway, in the blazing afternoon sun, and in about half a minute we heard wheels crunching the gravel. When the carriage stopped in front of the steps old Forster and I ran down.

'Great heaven, the carriage is empty! And yet---'

I had the door open in a minute, and this is what I saw . . .

No sign of John Charrington; and of May, his wife, only a huddled heap of white satin lying half on the floor of the carriage and half on the seat.

'I drove straight here, sir,' said the coachman, as the bride's father lifted her out; 'and I'll swear no one got out of the carriage.'

We carried her into the house in her bridal dress and drew back her veil. I saw her face. Shall I ever forget it? White, white and drawn with agony and horror, bearing such a look of terror as I have never seen since except in dreams. And her hair, her radiant blonde hair, I tell you it was white like snow.

As we stood, her father and I, half mad with the horror and mystery of it, a boy came up the avenue--a telegraph boy. They brought the orange envelope to me. I tore it open.

Mr Charrington was thrown from the dogcart on his way to the station at half past one. Killed on the spot!

And he was married to May Forster in our parish church at half past three, in presence of half the parish.

'I shall be married, dead, or alive!'

What had passed in that carriage on the homeward drive? No one knows--no one will ever know. Oh, May! oh, my dear!

Before a week was over they laid her beside her husband in our little churchyard on the thyme-covered hill--the churchyard where they had kept their love-trysts.

Thus was accomplished John Charrington's wedding.

THE END

In the Dark

by

Edith Nesbit

It may have been a form of madness. Or it may be that he really was what is called haunted. Or it may-though I don't pretend to understand how-have been the development, through intense suffering, of a sixth sense in a very nervous, highly strung nature. Something certainly led him where They were. And to him They were all one.

He told me the first part of the story, and the last part of it I saw with my own eyes.

Chapter I

Haldane and I were friends even in our school-days. What first brought us together was our common hatred of Visger, who came from our part of the country. His people knew our people at home, so he was put on to us when he came. He was the most intolerable person, boy and man, that I have ever known. He would not tell a lie. And that was all right. But he didn't stop at that. If he were asked whether any other chap had done anything-been out of bounds, or up to any sort of lark-he would always say, 'I don't know, sir, but I believe so. He never did know-we took care of that. But what he believed was always right. I remember Haldane twisting his arm to say how he knew about that cherry-tree business, and he only said, 'I don't know-I just feel sure. And I was right, you see.' What can you do with a boy like that?

We grew up to be men. At least Haldane and I did. Visger grew up to be a prig. He was a vegetarian and a teetotaller, and an all-wooler and Christian Scientist, and all the things that prigs are-but he wasn't a common prig. He knew all sorts of things that he oughtn't to have known, that he couldn't have known in any ordinary decent way. It wasn't that he found things out. He just knew them. Once, when I was very unhappy, he came into my rooms-we were all in our last year at Oxford-and talked about things I hardly knew myself. That was really why I went to India that winter. It was bad enough to be unhappy, without having that beast knowing all about it.

I was away over a year. Coming back, I thought a lot about how jolly it would be to see old Haldane again. If I thought about Visger at all, I wished he was dead. But I didn't think about him much.

I did want to see Haldane. He was always such a jolly chap-gay, and kindly, and simple, honourable, uptight, and full of practical sympathies. I longed to see him, to see the smile in his jolly blue eyes, looking out from the net of wrinkles that laughing had made round them, to hear his jolly laugh, and feel the good grip of his big hand. I went straight from the docks to his chambers in Gray's Inn, and I found him cold, pale, anaemic, with dull eyes and a limp hand, and pale lips that smiled without mirth, and uttered a welcome without gladness.

He was surrounded by a litter of disordered furniture and personal effects half packed. Some big boxes stood corded, and there were cases of books, filled and waiting for the enclosing boards to be nailed on.

'Yes, I'm moving,' he said. 'I can't stand these rooms. There's something rum about them--something devilish rum. I clear our tomorrow.'

The autumn dusk was filling the corners with shadows. 'You got the furs,' I said, just for something to say, for I saw the big case that held them lying corded among the others.

'Furs?' he said. 'Oh yes. Thanks awfully. Yes. I forgot about the furs.' He laughed, out of politeness, I suppose, for there was no joke about the furs. They were many and fine-the best I could get for money, and I had seen them packed and sent off when my heart was very sore. He stood looking at me, and saying nothing.

'Come out and have a bit of dinner,' I said as cheerfully as I could.

'Too busy,' he answered, after the slightest possible pause, and a glance round the room--'look here-I'm awfully glad to see you-If you'd just slip over and order in dinner-I'd go myself-only-Well, you see how it is.'

I went. And when I came back, he had cleared a space near the fire, and moved his big gate-table into it. We dined there by candle light. I tried to be amusing. He, I am sure, tried to be amused. We did not succeed, either of us. And his haggard eyes watched me all the time, save in those fleeting moments when, without turning his head, he glanced back over his shoulder into the shadows that crowded round the little lighted place where we sat.

When we had dined and the man had come and taken away the dishes, I looked at Haldane very steadily, so that he stopped in a pointless anecdote, and looked interrogatively at me. 'Well?' I said.

'You're not listening,' he said petulantly. 'What's the matter?'

'That's what you'd better tell me,' I said.

He was silent, gave one of those furtive glances at the shadows, and stooped to stir the fire to--I knew it-a blaze that must light every corner of the room.

'You're all to pieces,' I said cheerfully. 'What have you been up to? Wine? Cards? Speculation? A woman? If you won't tell me, you'll have to tell your doctor. Why, my dear chap, you're a wreck.'

'You're a comfortable friend to have about the place,' he said, and smiled a mechanical smile not at all pleasant to see.

'I'm the friend you want, I think,' said I. 'Do you suppose I'm blind? Something's gone wrong and you've taken to something. Morphia, perhaps? And you've brooded over the thing till you've lost all sense of proportion. Out with it, old chap. I bet you a dollar it's not so bad as you think it.'

'If I could tell you-or tell anyone,' he said slowly, 'it wouldn't be so bad as it is. If I could tell anyone, I'd tell you. And even as it is, I've told you more than I've told anyone else.'

I could get nothing more out of him. But he pressed me to stay-would have given me his bed and made himself a shake-down, he said. But I had engaged my room at the Victoria, and I was expecting letters. So I left him, quite late-and he stood on the stairs, holding a candle over the bannisters to light me down.

When I went back next morning, he was gone. Men were moving his furniture into a big van with somebody's Pantechnicon painted on it in big letters.

He had left no address with the porter, and had driven off in a hansom with two portmanteaux-to Waterloo, the porter thought.

Well, a man has a right to the monopoly of his own troubles, if he chooses to have it. And I had troubles of my own that kept me busy.

Chapter II

It was more than a year later that I saw Haldane again. I had got rooms in the Albany by this time, and he turned up there one morning, very early indeed-before breakfast in fact. And if he looked ghastly before, he now looked almost ghostly. His face looked as though it had worn thin, like an oyster shell that has for years been cast up twice a day by the sea on a shore all pebbly. His hands were thin as bird's claws, and they trembled like caught butterflies.

I welcomed him with enthusiastic cordiality and pressed breakfast on him. This time, I decided, I would ask no questions. For I saw that none were needed. He would tell me. He intended to tell me. He had come here to tell me, and for nothing else.

I lit the spirit lamp-I made coffee and small talk for him, and I ate and drank, and waited for him to begin. And it was like this that he began:

'I am going,' he said, 'to kill myself-oh, don't be alarmed,'-I suppose I had said or looked something-'I shan't do it here, or now. I shall do it when I have to-when I can't bear it any longer. And I want someone to know why. I don't want to feel that I'm the only living creature who does know. And I can trust you, can't I?'

I murmured something reassuring.

'I should like you, if you don't mind, to give me your word, that you won't tell a soul what I'm going to tell you, as long as I'm alive. Afterwards. . . you can tell whom you please.' I gave him my word.

He sat silent looking at the fire. Then he shrugged his shoulders.

'It's extraordinary how difficult it is to say it,' he said, and smiled. 'The fact is-you know that beast, George Visger.'

'Yes,' I said. 'I haven't seen him since I came back. Some one told me he'd gone to some island or other to preach vegetarianism to the cannibals. Anyhow, he's out of the way, bad luck to him.'

'Yes,' said Haldane, 'he's out of the way. But he's not preaching anything. In point of fact, he's dead.'

'Dead?' was all I could think of to say.

'Yes,' said he; 'it's not generally known, but he is.'

'What did he die of?' I asked, not that I cared. The bare fact was good enough for me.

'You know what an interfering chap he always was. Always knew everything. Heart to heart talks-and have everything open and above board. Well, he interfered between me and some one else-told her a pack of lies.'

'Lies?'

'Well, the things were true, but he made lies of them the way he told them-you know.' I did. I nodded. 'And she threw me over. And she died. And we weren't even friends. And I couldn't see her-before-I couldn't even. . . Oh, my God. . . But I went to the funeral. He was there. They'd asked him. And then I came back to my rooms. And I was sitting there, thinking. And he came up. 'He would do. It's just what he would do. The beast! I hope you kicked him out.'

'No, I didn't. I listened to what he'd got to say. He came to say, No doubt it was all for the best. And he hadn't known the things he told her. He'd only guessed. He'd guessed right, damn him. What right had he to guess right? And he said it was all for the best, because, besides that, there was madness in my family. He'd found that out too-'

'And is there?'

'If there is, I didn't know it. And that was why it was all for the best. So then I said, "There wasn't any madness in my family before, but there is now," and I got hold of his throat. I am not sure whether I meant to kill him; I ought to have meant to kill him. Anyhow, I did kill him. What did you say?'

I had said nothing. It is not easy to think at once of the tactful and suitable thing to say, when your oldest friend tells you that he is a murderer.

'When I could get my hands out of his throat-it was as difficult as it is to drop the handles of a galvanic battery-he fell in a lump on the hearth-rug. And I saw what I'd done. How is it that murderers ever get found out?'

'They're careless, I suppose,' I found myself saying, 'they lose their nerve.'

'I didn't,' he said. 'I never was calmer, I sat down in the big chair and looked at him, and thought it all out. He was just off to that island--I knew that. He'd said goodbye to everyone. He'd told me that. There was no blood to get rid of-or only a touch at the corner of his slack mouth. He wasn't going to travel in his own name because of interviewers. Mr Somebody Something's luggage would be unclaimed and his cabin empty. No one would guess that Mr Somebody Something was Sir George Visger, FRS. It was all as plain as plain. There was nothing to get rid of, but the man. No weapon, no blood-and I got rid of him all right.'

'How?'

He smiled cunningly.

'No, no,' he said; 'that's where I draw the line. It's not that I doubt your word, but if you talked in your sleep, or had a fever or anything. No, no. As long as you don't know where the body is, don't you see, I'm all right. Even if you could prove that I've said all this-which you can't--it's only the wanderings of my poor unhinged brain. See?'

I saw. And I was sorry for him. And I did not believe that he had killed Visger. He was not the sort of man who kills people. So I said:

'Yes, old chap, I see. Now look here. Let's go away together, you and I-travel a bit and see the world, and forget all about that beastly chap.'

His eyes lighted up at that.

'Why,' he said, 'you understand. You don't hate me and shrink from me. I wish I'd told you before-you know-when you came and I was packing all my sticks. But it's too late now.

'Too late? Not a bit of it,' I said. 'Come, we'll pack our traps and be off tonight-out into the unknown, don't you know.

'That's where I'm going,' he said. 'You wait. When you've heard what's been happening to me, you won't be so keen to go travelling about with me.'

'But you've told me what's been happening to you,' I said, and the more I thought about what he had told me, the less I believed it.

'No,' he said, slowly, 'no-I've told you what happened to him. What happened to me is quite different. Did I tell you what his last words were? Just when I was coming at him. Before I'd got his throat, you know. He said, "Look out. You'll never to able to get rid of the body-Besides, anger's sinful." You know that way he had, like a tract on its hind legs. So afterwards I got thinking of that. But I didn't think of it for a year. Because I did get rid of his body all right. And then I was sitting in that comfortable chair, and I thought, "Hullo, it must be about a year now, since that-" and I pulled out my pocket-book and went to the window to look at a little almanac I carry about-it was getting dusk-and sure enough it was a year, to the day. And then I remembered what he'd said. And I said to myself, "Not much trouble about getting rid of your body, you brute." And then I looked at the hearth-rug and-Ah!' he screamed suddenly and very loud-'I can't tell you-no, I can't.'

My man opened the door-he wore a smooth face over his wriggling curiosity. 'Did you call, sir?'

'Yes,' I lied. 'I want you to take a note to the bank, and wait for an answer.'

When he was got rid of, Haldane said: 'Where was I?-'

'You were just telling me what happened after you looked at the almanac. What was it?'

'Nothing much,' he said, laughing softly, 'oh, nothing much-only that I glanced at the hearthrug-and there he was-the man I'd killed a year before. Don't try to explain, or I shall lose my temper. The door was shut. The windows were shut. He hadn't been there a minute before. And he was there then. That's all.'

Hallucination was one of the words I stumbled among.

'Exactly what I thought,' he said triumphantly, 'but-I touched it. It was quite real. Heavy, you know, and harder than live people are somehow, to the touch-more like a stone thing covered with kid the hands were, and the arms like a marble statue in a blue serge suit. Don't you hate men who wear blue serge suits?' 'There are hallucinations of touch too,' I found myself saying..

'Exactly what I thought,' said Haldane more triumphant than ever, 'but there are limits, you know-limits. So then I thought someone had got him out-the real him-and stuck him there to frighten me-while my back was turned, and I went to the place where I'd hidden him, and he was there-ah!-just as I'd left him. Only. . . it was a year ago. There are two of him there now.'

'My dear chap,' I said 'this is simply comic.'

'Yes,' he said, 'It is amusing. I find it so myself. Especially in the night when I wake up and think of it. I hope I shan't die in the dark, Winston: That's one of the reasons why I think I shall have to kill myself. I could be sure then of not dying in the dark.'

'Is that all?' I asked, feeling sure that it must be.

'No,' said Haldane at once. 'That's not all. He's come back to rue again. In a railway carriage it was. I'd been asleep. When I woke up, there he was lying on the seat opposite me. Looked just the same. I pitched him out on the line in Red Hill Tunnel. And if I see him again, I'm going out myself. I can't stand it. It's too much. I'd sooner go. Whatever the next world's like, there aren't things in it like that. We leave them here, in graves and boxes and . . You think I'm mad. But I'm not. You can't help me-no one can help me. He knew, you see. He said I shouldn't be able to get rid of the body. And I can't get rid of it. I can't. I can't. He knew. He always did know things that he couldn't know. But I'll cut his game short. After all, I've got the ace of trumps, and I'll play it on his next trick. I give you my word of honour, Winston, that I'm not mad.'

'My dear old man,' I said, 'I don't think you're mad. But I do think your nerves are very much upset. Mine are a bit, too. Do you know why I went to India? It was because of you and her. I couldn't stay and see it, though I wished for your happiness and all that; you know I did. And when I came back, she . . . and you . . . Let's see it out together,' I said. 'You won't keep fancying things if you've got me to talk to. And I always said you weren't half a bad old duffer.'

'She liked you,' he said.

'Oh, yes,' I said, 'she liked me.

Chapter III

That was how we came to go abroad together. I was full of hope for him. He'd always been such a splendid chap-so sane and strong. I couldn't believe that he was gone mad, gone for ever, I mean, so that he'd never come right again. Perhaps may own trouble made it easy for me to see things not quite straight. Anyway, I took him away to recover his mind's health, exactly as I should have taken him away to get strong after a fever. And the madness seemed to pass away, and in a month or two we were perfectly jolly, and I thought I had cured him. And I was very glad because of that old friendship of ours, and because she had loved him and liked me.

We never spoke of Visger. I thought he had forgotten all about him. I thought I understood how his mind, over-strained by sorrow and anger, had fixed on the man he hated, and woven a nightmare web of horror round that detestable personality. And I had got the whip hand of my own trouble. And we were as jolly as sandboys together all those months.

And we came to Bruges at last in our travels, and Bruges was very full, because of the Exhibition. We could only get one room and one bed. So we tossed for the bed, and the one who lost the toss was to make the best of the night in the armchair. And the bedclothes we were to share equitably.

We spent the evening at a café chantant and finished at a beer hall, and it was late and sleepy when we got back to the Grande Vigne. I took our key from its nail in the concierge's room, and we went up. We talked awhile, I remember, of the town, and the belfry, and the Venetian aspect of the canals by moonlight, and then Haldane got into bed, and I made a chrysalis of myself with my share of the blankets and fitted the tight roll into the armchair. I was not at all comfortable, but I was compensatingly tired, and I was nearly asleep when Haldane roused me up to tell me about his will.

'I've left everything to you, old man,' he said. 'I know I can trust you to see to everything.' 'Quite so,' said I, 'and if you don't mind, we'll talk about it in the morning.'

He tried to go on about it, and about what a friend I'd been, and all that, but I shut him up and told him to go to sleep. But no. He wasn't comfortable, he said. And he'd got a thirst like a lime kiln. And he'd noticed that there was no water-bottle in the room. 'And the water in the jug's like pale soup,' he said.

'Oh, all right,' said I. 'Light your candle and go and get some water, then, in Heaven's name, and let me get to sleep.'

But he said, 'No-you light it. I don't want to get out of bed in the dark. I might-I might step on something, mightn't I-or walk into something that wasn't there when I got into bed.'

'Rot,' I said, 'walk into your grandmother.' But I lit the candle all the same. He sat up in bed and looked at me-very pale-with his hair all tumbled from the pillow, and his eyes blinking and shining/ 'That's better,' he said. And then, 'I say-look here. Oh-yes-I see. It's all right. Queer how they mark the sheets here. Blest if I didn't think it was blood, just for the minute.' The sheet was marked, not at the corner, as sheets are marked at home, but right in the middle where it turns down, with big, red, cross-stitching.

'Yes, I see,' I said, 'it is a queer place to mark it.'

'It's queer letters to have on it,' he said. 'G.V.'

'Grande Vigne,' I said. 'What letters do you expect them to mark things with? Hurry up.

'You come too,' he said. 'Yes, it does stand for Grande Vigne, of course. I wish you'd come down too, Winston.'

'I'll go down,' I said and turned with the candle in my hand.

He was out of bed and close to me in a flash.

'No,' said he, 'I don't want to stay alone in the dark.'

He said it just as a frightened child might have done.

'All right then, come along,' I said. And we went. I tried to make some joke, I remember, about the length of his hair, and the cut of his pyjamas-but I was sick with disappointment. For it was almost quite plain to me, even then, that all my time and trouble had been thrown away, and that he wasn't cured after all. We went down as quietly as we could, and got a carafe of water from the long bare dining table in the sale à manger. He got hold of my arm at first, and then he got the candle away from me, and went very slowly, shading the light with his hand, and looking very carefully all about, as though he expected to see something that he wanted very desperately nor to see. And of course, I knew what that something was. I didn't like the way he was going on. I can't at all express how deeply I didn't like it. And he looked over his shoulder every now and then, just as he did that first evening after I came back from India.

The thing got on my nerves so that I could hardly find the way back to our room. And when we got there, I give you my word, I more than half expected to see what he had expected to see--that, or something like that, on the hearth-rug. But of course there was nothing.

I blew out the light and tightened my blankets round me-I'd been trailing them after me in our expedition. And I was settled in my chair when Haldane spoke.

'You've got all the blankets,' he said.

'No, I haven't,' said I, 'only what I've always had.' 'I can't find mine then,' he said and I could hear his teeth chattering. 'And I'm cold. I'm. . .

For God's sake, light the candle. Light it. Light it. Something horrible. . .'

And I couldn't find the matches.

'Light the candle, light the candle,' he said, and his voice broke, as a boy's does sometimes in chapel. 'If you don't he'll come to me. It is so easy to come at any one in the dark. Oh Winston, light the candle, for the love of God! I can't die in the dark.'

'I am lighting it,' I said savagely, and I was feeling for the matches on the marble-topped chest of drawers, on the mantelpiece-everywhere but on the round centre table where I'd put them. 'You're not going to die. Don't be a fool,' I said. 'It's all right. I'll get a light in a second.'

He said, 'It's cold. It's cold. It's cold,' like that, three times. And then he screamed aloud, like a woman-like a child-like a hare when the dogs have got it. I had heard him scream like that once before.

'What is it?' I cried, hardly less loud. 'For God's sake, hold your noise. What is it?' There was an empty silence. Then, very slowly:

'It's Visger,' he said. And he spoke thickly, as through some stifling veil.

'Nonsense. Where?' I asked, and my hand closed on the matches as he spoke.

'Here,' he screamed sharply, as though he had torn the veil away, 'here, beside me. In the bed.' I got the candle alight. I got across to him.

He was crushed in a heap at the edge of the bed. Stretched on the bed beyond him was a dead man, white and very cold.

Haldane had died in the dark.

It was all so simple.

We had come to the wrong room. The man the room belonged to was there, on the bed he had engaged and paid for before he died of heart disease, earlier in the day. A French commis-voyageur representing soap and perfumery; his name, Felix Leblanc.

Later, in England, I made cautious enquiries. The body of a man had been found in the Red Hill tunnel-a haberdasher man named Simmons, who had drunk spirits of salts, owing to the depression of trade. The bottle was clutched in his dead hand.

For reasons that I had, I took care to have a police inspector with me when I opened the boxes that came to me by Haldane's will. One of them was the big box, metal lined, in which I had sent him the skins from India-for a wedding present, God help us all!

It was closely soldered.

Inside were the skins of beasts? No. The bodies of two men. One was identified, after some trouble, as that of a hawker of pens in city offices-subject to fits. He had died in one, it seemed. The other body was Visger's, right enough.

Explain it as you like. I offered you, if you remember, a choice of explanations before I began the story. I have not yet found the explanation that can satisfy me.

THE END

The Mystery of the Semi-Detached

by

Edith Nesbit

He was waiting for her, he had been waiting an hour and a half in a dusty suburban lane, with a row of big elms on one side and some eligible building sites on the other-and far away to the south-west the twinkling yellow lights of the Crystal Palace. It was not quite like a country lane, for it had a pavement and lamp-posts, but it was not a bad place for a meeting all the same: and farther up, towards the cemetery, it was really quite rural, and almost pretty, especially in twilight But twilight had long deepened into the night, and still he waited. He loved her, and he was engaged to be married to her, with the complete disapproval of every reasonable person who had been consulted. And this half-clandestine meeting was tonight to take the place of the grudgingly sanctioned weekly interview-because a certain rich uncle was visiting at her house, and her mother was not the woman to acknowledge to a moneyed uncle, who might "go off" any day, a match so deeply ineligible as hers with him.

So he waited for her, and the chill of an unusually severe May evening entered into his bones.

The policeman passed him with a surly response to his "Good night". The bicyclists went by him like grey ghosts with foghorns; and it was nearly ten o'clock, and she had not come.

He shrugged his shoulders and turned towards his lodgings. His road led him by her house--desirable, commodious, semi-detached-and he walked slowly as he neared it She might, even now, be coming out But she was not There was no sign of movement about the house, no sign of life, no lights even in the windows. And her people were not early people.

He paused by the gate, wondering.

Then he noticed that the front door was open-wide open-and the street lamp shone a little way into the dark hail. There was something about all this that did not please him-that scared him a little, indeed. The house had a gloomy and deserted air. It was obviously impossible that it harboured a rich uncle. The old man must have left early. In which case-

He walked up the path of patent glazed dies, and listened. No sign of life. He passed into the hail. There was no light anywhere. Where was everybody, and why was the front door open? There was no one in the drawing room, the dining room and the study (nine feet by seven) were equally blank. Everyone was out, evidently. But the unpleasant sense that he was, perhaps, not the first casual visitor to walk through that open door impelled him to look through the house before he went away and closed it after him. So he went upstairs, and at the door of the first bedroom he came to he struck a wax match, as he had done in the sitting rooms. Even as he did so he felt that he was not alone. And he was prepared to see something but for what he saw he was not prepared. For what he saw lay on the bed, in a white loose gown-and it was his sweetheart, and its throat was cut from ear to ear. He doesn't know what happened then, nor how he got downstairs and into the street; but he got out somehow, and the policeman found him in a fit, under the lamp-post at the corner of the street He couldn't speak when they picked him up, and he passed the night in the police cells, because the policeman had seen plenty of drunken men before, but never one in a fit.

The next morning he was better, though still very white and shaky. But the tale he told the magistrate was convincing, and they sent a couple of constables with him to her house.

There was no crowd about it as he had fancied there would be, and the blinds were not down.

He held on to the door-post for support...

"She's all right, you see," said the constable, who had found him under the lamp. "I told you you was drunk, but you would know best-"

When he was alone with her he told her-not all-for that would not bear telling-but how he had come into the commodious semi-detached, and how he had found the door open and the lights out, and that he had been into that long back room facing the stairs, and had seen something-in even trying to hint at which he turned sick and broke down and had to have brandy given him.

"But, my dearest," she said, "I dare say the house was dark, for we were all at the Crystal Palace with my uncle, and no doubt the door was open, for the maids will run out if they're left. But you could not have been in that room, because I locked it when I came away, and the key was in my pocket. I dressed in a hurry and I left all my odds and ends lying about."

"I know," he said; "I saw a green scarf on a chair, and some long brown gloves, and a lot of hairpins and ribbons, and a prayerbook, and a lace handkerchief on the dressing table. Why, I even noticed the almanac on the mantelpiece-21 October. At least it couldn't be that, because this is May. And yet it was. Your almanac is at 21 October, isn't it?"

"No, of course it isn't," she said, smiling rather anxiously; "but all the other things were just as you say. You must have had a dream, or a vision, or something."

He was a very ordinary, commonplace, City young man, and he didn't believe in visions, but he never rested day or night till he got his sweetheart and her mother away from that commodious semi-detached, and settled them in a quiet distant suburb. In the course of the removal he incidentally married her, and the mother went on living with them.

His nerves must have been a good bit shaken, because he was very queer for a long time, and was always enquiring if anyone had taken the desirable semi-detached; and when an old stockbroker with a family took it, he went the length of calling on the old gentleman and imploring him by all that he held dear, not to live in that fatal house.

"Why?" said the stockbroker, not unnaturally.

And then he got so vague and confused, between trying to tell why and trying not to tell why, that the stockbroker showed him out, and thanked his God he was not such a fool as to allow a lunatic to stand in the way of his taking that really remarkably cheap and desirable semi-detached residence.

Now the curious and quite inexplicable part of this story is that when she came down to breakfast on the morning of the 22 October she found him looking like death, with the morning paper in his hand. He caught hers--he couldn't speak, and pointed to the paper. And there she read that on the night of the 21st a young lady, the stockbroker's daughter, had been found, with her throat cut from ear to ear, on the bed in the long back bedroom facing the stairs of that desirable semi-detached.

THE END

The Ebony Frame

by

Edith Nesbit

To be rich is a luxurious sensation, the more so when you have plumbed the depths of hard-up-ness as a Fleet Street hack, a picker-up of unconsidered pars, a reporter, an unappreciated journalist; all callings utterly inconsistent with one's family feeling and one's direct descent from the Dukes of Picardy.

When my Aunt Dorcas died and left me seven hundred a year and a furnished house in Chelsea, I felt that life had nothing left to offer except immediate possession of the legacy. Even Mildred Mayhew, whom I had hitherto regarded as my life's light, became less luminous. I was not engaged to Mildred, but I lodged with her mother, and I sang duets with Mildred and gave her gloves when it would run to it, which was seldom. She was a dear, good girl, and I meant to marry her some day. It is very nice to feel that a good little woman is thinking of you? it helps you in your work? and it is pleasant to know she will say "Yes," when you say, "Will you?"

But my legacy almost put Mildred out of my head, especially as she was staying with friends in the country.

Before the gloss was off my new mourning, I was seated in my aunt's armchair in front of the fire in the drawing-room of my own house. My own house! It was grand, but rather lonely. I did think of Mildred just then.

The room was comfortably furnished with rosewood and damask. On the walls hung a few fairly good oil paintings, but the space above the mantelpiece was disfigured by an exceedingly bad print, "The Trial of Lord William Russell," framed in a dark frame. I got up to look at it. I had visited my aunt with dutiful regularity, but I never remembered seeing this frame before. It was not intended for a print, but for an oil-painting. It was of fine ebony, beautifully and curiously carved. I looked at it with growing interest, and when my aunt's housemaid? I had retained her modest staff of servants? came in with the lamp, I asked her how long the print had been there.

"Mistress only bought it two days before she was took ill," she said; "but the frame? she didn't want to buy a new one? so she got this out of the attic. There's lots of curious old things there, sir."

"Had my aunt had this frame long?"

"Oh, yes, sir. It must have come long before I did, and I've been here seven years come Christmas. There was a picture in it. That's upstairs too? but it's that black and ugly it might as well be a chimney-back."

I felt a desire to see this picture. What if it were some priceless old master, in which my aunt's eyes had only seen rubbish?

Directly after breakfast next morning, I paid a visit to the attic.

It was crammed with old furniture enough to stock a curiosity shop. All the house was furnished solidly in the Mid-Victorian style, and in this room everything not in keeping with the drawing-room suite ideal was stowed away. Tables of papier-mâché and mother-of-pearl, straight-backed chairs with twisted feet and faded needle-work cushions, fire-screens of gilded carving and beaded banners, oak bureaux with brass handles, a little worktable with its faded, moth-eaten, silk flutings hanging in disconsolate shreds; on these, and the dust that covered them, blazed the full daylight as I pulled up the blinds. I promised myself a good time in re-enshrining these household gods in my parlour, and promoting the Victorian suite to the attic. But at present my business was to find the picture as "black as the chimney back"; and presently, behind a heap of fenders and boxes, I found it.

Jane, the housemaid, identified it at once. I took it downstairs carefully, and examined it. Neither subject nor colour was distinguishable. There was a splodge of a darker tint in the middle, but whether it was figure, or tree, or house, no man could have told. It seemed to be painted on a very thick panel bound with leather. I decided to send it to one of those persons who pour on rotting family portraits the water of eternal youth; but even as I did so, I thought, why not try my own restorative hand at a corner of it.

My bath-sponge soap and nail-brush, vigorously applied for a few seconds, showed me that there was no picture to clean. Bare oak presented itself to my persevering brush. I tried the other side, Jane watching me with indulgent interest. The same result. Then the truth dawned on me. Why was the panel so thick? I tore off the leather binding, and the panel divided and fell to the ground in a cloud of dust. There were two pictures, they had been nailed face to face. I leaned them against the wall, and the next moment I was leaning against it myself.

For one of the pictures was myself, a perfect portrait, no shade of expression or turn of feature wanting. Myself, in the dress men wore when James the First was King. When had this been done? And how, without my knowledge? Was this some whim of my aunt's?

"Lor', sir!" the shrill surprise of Jane at my elbow; "what a lovely photo it is! Was it a fancy ball, sir?"

"Yes," I stammered. "I? I don't think I want anything more now. You can go."

She went; and I turned, still with my heart beating violently, to the other picture. This was a beautiful woman's picture, very beautiful she was. I noted all her beauties, straight nose, low brows, full lips, thin hands, large, deep, luminous eyes. She wore a black velvet gown. It was a three-quarter-length portrait. Her arms rested on a table beside her, and her head on her hands; but her face was turned full forward, and her eyes met those of the spectator bewilderingly. On the table by her were compasses and shining instruments whose uses I did not know, books, a goblet, and a heap of papers and pens. I saw all this afterwards. I believe it was a quarter of an hour before I could turn my eyes from her. I have never see any other eyes like hers; they appealed, as a child's or a dog's do; they commanded, as might those of an empress.

"Shall I sweep up the dust sir?" Curiosity had brought Jane back. I acceded. I turned from her my portrait. I kept between her and the woman in the black velvet. When I was alone again I tore down "The Trial of Lord William Russell," and I put the picture of the woman in its strong ebony frame.

Then I wrote to a frame-maker for a frame for my portrait. It had so long lived face to face with this beautiful witch that I had not the heart to banish it from her presence; I suppose I am sentimental, if it be sentimental to think such things as that.

The new frame came home, and I hung it opposite the fireplace. An exhaustive search among my aunt's papers showed no explanation of the portrait of myself, no history of the portrait of the woman with the wonderful eyes. I only learned that all the old furniture together had come to my aunt at the death of my great-uncle, the head of the family;

and I should have concluded that the resemblance was only a family one, if everyone who came in had not exclaimed at the "speaking likeness." I adopted Jane's "fancy ball" explanation.

And there, one might suppose, the matter of the portraits ended. One might suppose it, that is, if there were not evidently a good deal more written here about it. However, to me then the matter seemed ended.

I went to see Mildred; I invited her and her mother to come and stay with me; I rather avoided glancing at the picture in ebony frame. I could not forget, nor remember without singular emotion, the look in the eyes of that woman when mine first met them. I shrank from meeting that look again.

I reorganised the house somewhat, preparing for Mildred's visit. I brought down much of the old-fashioned furniture, and after a long day of arranging and re-arranging, I sat down before the fire, and lying back in a pleasant languor, I idly raised my eyes to the picture of the woman. I met her dark, deep, hazel eyes, and once more my gaze was held fixed as by strong magic, the kind of fascination that keeps one sometimes staring for whole minutes into one's own eyes in the glass. I gazed into her eyes, and felt my own dilate, pricked with a smart like the smart of tears.

"I wish," I said, "oh, how I wish you were a woman and not a picture! Come down! Ah, come down!"

I laughed at myself as I spoke; but even as I laughed, I held out my arms.

I was not sleepy; I was not drunk. I was as wide awake and as sober as ever was a man in the world. And yet, as I held out my arms, I saw the eyes of the picture dilate, her lips tremble? If I were to be hanged for saying it, it is true.

Her hands moved slightly; and a sort of flicker of a smile passed over her face.

I sprang to my feet. "This won't do," I said aloud. "Firelight does play strange tricks. I'll have the lamp."

I made for the bell. My hand was on it, when I heard a sound behind me, and turned, the bell still unrung. The fire had burned low and the corners of the room were deeply shadowed; but surely, there, behind the tall worked chair, was something darker than a shadow.

"I must face this out," I said, "or I shall never be able to face myself again." I left the bell, I seized the poker, and battered the dull coals to a blaze. Then I stepped back resolutely, and looked at the picture. The ebony frame was empty! From the shadow of the worked chair came a soft rustle, and out of the shadow the woman of the picture was coming, coming towards me.

I hope I shall never again know a moment of terror as blank and absolute. I could not have moved or spoken to save my life. Either all the known laws of nature were nothing, or I was mad. I stood trembling, but, I am thankful to remember, I stood still, while the black velvet gown swept across the hearthrug towards me.

Next moment a hand touched me, a hand, soft, warm, and human, and a low voice said, "You called me. I am here."

At that touch and that voice, the world seemed to give a sort of bewildering half-turn. I hardly know how to express it, but at once it seemed not awful, not even unusual, for portraits to become flesh, only most natural, most right, most unspeakably fortunate.

I laid my hand on hers. I looked from her to my portrait. I could not see it in the firelight. "We are not strangers," I said.

"Oh, no, not strangers." Those luminous eyes were looking up into mine, those red lips were near me. With a passionate cry, a sense of having recovered life's one great good, that had seemed wholly lost, I clasped her in my arms. She was no ghost, she was a woman, the only woman in the world.

"How long," I said, "how long is it since I lost you?"

She leaned back, hanging her full weight on the hands that were clasped behind my head. "How can I tell how long? There is no time in hell," she answered.

It was not a dream. Ah! no? there are no such dreams. I wish to God there could be. When in dreams do I see her eyes, hear her voice, feel her lips against my cheek, hold her hands to my lips, as I did that night, the supreme night of my life! At first we hardly spoke. It seemed enough:

after long grief and pain.

To feel the arms of my true love.

Round me once again.

It is very difficult to tell my story. There are no words to express the sense of glad reunion, the complete realisation of every hope and dream of a life, that came upon me as I sat with my hand in hers, and looked into her eyes.

How could it have been a dream, when I left her sitting in the straight-backed chair, and went down to the kitchen to tell the maids I should want nothing more, that I was busy, and did not wish to be disturbed; when I fetched wood for the fire with my own hands, and, bringing it in, found her still sitting there, saw the little brown head turn as I entered, saw the love in her dear eyes; when I threw myself at her feet and blessed the day I was born, since life had given me this.

Not a thought of Mildred; all other things in my life were a dream, this, its one splendid reality.

"I am wondering," she said, after a while, when we had made such cheer, each of the other, as true lovers may after long parting, "I am wondering how much you remember of our past?"

"I remember nothing but that I love you, that I have loved you all my life."

"You remember nothing? Really nothing?"

"Only that I am truly yours; that we have both suffered; that, tell me, my mistress dear, all that you remember. Explain it all to me. Make me understand. And yet? No, I don't want to understand. It is enough that we are together."

If it was a dream, why have I never dreamed it again?

She leaned down towards me, her arm lay on my neck, and drew my head till it rested on her shoulder. "I am a ghost, I suppose," she said, laughing softly; and her laughter stirred memories which I just grasped at and just missed. "But you and I know better, don't we? I will tell you everything you have forgotten. We loved each other, ah! no, you have not forgotten that, and when you came back from the wars, we were to be married. Our pictures were painted before you went away. You know I was more learned than women of that day. Dear one, when you were gone, they said I was a witch. They tried me. They said I should be burned. Just because I had looked at the stars and gained more knowledge than other women, they must needs bind me to a stake and let me be eaten by the fire. And you far away!"

Her whole body trembled and shrank. Oh love, what dream would have told me that my kisses would soothe even that memory?

"The night before," she went on, "the devil did come to me. I was innocent before, you know it, don't you? And even then my sin was for you! for you! because of the exceeding love I bore you! The devil came, and I sold my soul to eternal flame. But I got a good price. I got the right to come back through my picture (if anyone, looking at it, wished for me), as long as my picture stayed in its ebony frame. That frame was not carved by man's hand. I got the right to come back to you, oh, my heart's heart. And another thing I won, which you shall hear anon. They burned me for a witch, they made me suffer hell on earth. Those faces, all crowding round, the crackling wood and the choking smell of the smoke!"

"Oh, love, no more, no more!"

"When my mother sat that night before my picture, she wept and cried, 'Come back, my poor, lost child!' And I went to her with glad leaps of heart. Dear, she shrank from me, she fled, she shrieked and moaned of ghosts. She had our pictures covered from sight, and put again in the ebony frame. She had promised me my picture should stay always there. Ah, through all these years your face was against mine."

She paused.

"But the man you loved?"

"You came home. My picture was gone. They lied to you, and you married another woman; but some day I knew you would walk the world again, and that I should find you."

"The other gain?" I asked.

"The other gain," she said slowly, "I gave my soul for. It is this. If you also will give up your hopes of heaven, I can remain a woman, I can remain in your world! I can be your wife. Oh my dear, after all these years, at last! at last!"

"If I sacrifice my soul," I said slowly, and the words did not seem an imbecility, "if I sacrifice my soul I win you? Why, love, it's a contradiction in terms. You are my soul."

Her eyes looked straight into mine. Whatever might happen, whatever did happen, whatever may happen, our two souls in that moment met and became one.

"Then you choose, you deliberately choose, to give up your hopes of heaven for me, as I gave up mine for you?"

"I will not," I said, "give up my hope of heaven on any terms. Tell me what I must do that you and I may make our heaven here, as now?"

"I will tell you to-morrow," she said. "Be alone here to-morrow night, twelve is ghost's time, isn't it? And then I will come out of the picture, and never go back to it. I shall live with you, and die, and be buried, and there will be an end of me. But we shall live first, my heart's heart."

I laid my head on her knee. A strange drowsiness overcame me. Holding her hand against my cheek, I lost consciousness. When I awoke, the grey November dawn was glimmering, ghost like, through the uncurtained window. My head was pillowed on my arm, and rested. I raised my head quickly, ah! not on my lady's knee, but on the needle-worked cushion of the straight-backed chair. I sprang to my feet. I was stiff with cold and dazed with dreams, but I turned my eyes on the picture.. There she sat, my lady, my dear love. I held out my arms, but the passionate cry I would have uttered died on my lips. She had said twelve o'clock. Her lightest word was my law. So I only stood in front of the picture, and gazed into those grey-green eyes till tears of passionate happiness filled my own.

"Oh! my dear, my dear, how shall I pass the hours till I hold you again?"

No thought, then, of my whole life's completion and consummation being a dream.

I staggered up to my room, fell across my bed, and slept heavily and dreamlessly. When I awoke it was high noon. Mildred and her mother were coming to lunch.

I remembered, at one o'clock, Mildred coming and her existence.

Now indeed the dream began.

With a penetrating sense of the futility of any action apart from her, I gave the necessary orders for the reception of my guests. When Mildred and her mother came I received them with cordiality; but my genial phrases all seemed to be someone else's. My voice sounded like an echo; my heart was not there.

Still, the situation was not intolerable, until the hour when afternoon tea was served in the drawing-room. Mildred and mother kept the conversational pot boiling with a profusion of genteel commonplaces, and I bore it, as one in sight of heaven can bear mild purgatory. I looked up at my sweetheart in the ebony frame, and I felt that anything which might happen, any irresponsible imbecility, any bathos of boredom, was nothing, if, after all, she came to me again.

And yet, when Mildred, too, looked at the portrait and said: "Doesn't she think a lot of herself? Theatrical character, I suppose? One of your flames, Mr. Devigne?" I had a sickening sense of impotent irritation which became absolute torture when Mildred, (how could I ever have admired that chocolate-box barmaid style of prettiness) threw herself into the high-backed chair, covering the needlework with ridiculous flounces, and added, "Silence gives consent! Who is it, Mr. Devigne? Tell us all about her: I am sure she has a story."

Poor little Mildred, sitting there smiling, serene in her confidence that her every word charmed me, sitting there with her rather pinched waist, her rather tight boots, her rather vulgar voice, sitting in the chair where my dear lady had sat when she told me her story! I could not bear it.

"Don't sit there," I said, "it's not comfortable!"

But the girl would not be warned. With a laugh that set every nerve in my body vibrating with annoyance, she said, "Oh, dear! mustn't I even sit in the same chair as your black-velvet woman?"

I looked at the chair in the picture. It was the same, and in her chair Mildred was sitting. Then a horrible sense of the reality of Mildred came upon me, Was all this a reality after all? But for fortunate chance, might Mildred have occupied, not only her chair, but her place in my life? I rose.

"I hope you won't think me very rude," I said, "but I am obliged to go out."

I forget what appointment I alleged. The lie came readily enough.

I faced Mildred's pouts with the hope that she and her mother would not wait dinner for me. I fled. In another minute I was safe, alone, under the chill, cloudy, autumn sky-free to think, think, think of my dear lady.

I walked for hours along streets and squares; I lived over and over again every look, word and hand-touch, every kiss; I was completely, unspeakably happy.

Mildred was utterly forgotten; my lady of the ebony frame filled my heart, and soul, and spirit.

As I heard eleven boom through the fog, I turned and went home.

When I got to my street, I found a crowd surging through it, a strong red, light filling the air.

A house was on fire. Mine!

I elbowed my way through the crowd.

The picture of my lady, that, at least, I could save.

As I sprang up the steps, I saw, as in a dream, yes, all this was really dream-like, I saw Mildred leaning out of the first-floor window, wringing her hands.

"Come back, sir," cried a fireman; "we'll get the young lady out right enough."

But my lady? The stairs were crackling, smoking, and as hot as hell. I went up to the room where her picture was. Strange to say, I only felt that the picture was a thing we should like to look on through the long, glad, wedded life that was to be ours. I never thought of it as being one with her.

As I reached the first floor I felt arms about my neck. The smoke was too thick for me to distinguish features.

"Save me," a voice whispered. I clasped a figure in my arms and bore it with a strange disease, down the shaking stairs and out into safety. It was Mildred. I knew that directly I clasped her.

"Stand back," cried the crowd.

"Everyone's safe," cried a fireman.

The flames leaped from every window The sky grew redder and redder. I sprang from the hands that would have held me. I leaped up the steps. I crawled up the stairs. Suddenly the whole horror came to me. "As long as my picture remains in the ebony frame." What if picture and frame perished together?

I fought with the fire and with my own choking inability to fight with it. I pushed on. I must save my picture. I reached the drawing room.

As I sprang in, I saw my lady, I swear it, through the smoke and the flames, hold out her arms to me, to me, who came too late to save her, and to save my own life's joy. I never saw her again.

Before I could reach her, or cry out to her, I felt the floor yield beneath my feet, and I fell into the flames below.

How did they save me? What does that matter? They saved me somehow, curse them. Every stick of my aunt's furniture was destroyed. My friends pointed out that, as the furniture was heavily insured, the carelessness of a nightly-studious housemaid had done me no harm.

No harm!

That was how I won and lost my only love.

I deny, with all my soul in the denial, that it was a dream. There are no such dreams. Dreams of longing and pain there are in plenty; but dreams of complete, of unspeakable happiness? ah, no? it is the rest of life that is the dream.

But, if I think that, why have I married Mildred and grown stout, and dull, and prosperous?

I tell you, it is all this that is the dream; my dear lady only is the reality. And what does it matter what one does in a dream?

THE END

Collected Ghost Stories - 22 stories
M. R. James
Benediction Classics, 2011
284 pages
ISBN: 978-1-84902-454-9

Available from www.amazon.com, www.amazon.co.uk

Collected Ghost Stories by M R James is a collection of twenty-two ghost stories, plus a fascinating essay on the writing of ghost stories. Montague Rhodes James (1862-1936) was a medieval scholar and Provost of King's College, Cambridge. His stories are classics of their genre, understated, beautifully paced and almost never explicit. Their idyllic rural backgrounds and amiable hero make the chilling terror of otherworldly intrusions all the more horrific. The collection is comprised of the following twenty-two stories: The Uncommon Prayer-Book; A Neighbour's Landmark; Rats; The Experiment; The Malice Of Inanimate Objects; A Vignette; Canon Alberic's Scrap-Book; The Stalls Of Barchester Cathedral; An Episode Of Cathedral History; The Story Of A Disappearance And An Appearance; The Haunted Dolls' House; Lost Hearts; Mr. Humphreys And His Inheritance; Martin's Close; The Diary Of Mr. Poynter; The Rose-Garden; Casting The Runes; A School Story; The Tractate Middoth; Two Doctors; A View From A Hill; The Residence At Whitminster; Appendix: M. R. James On Ghost Stories Note: This is not to be confused with the Book "The Collected Ghost Stories of M R James" which was published in 1931.

Collected Twilight Stories - 18 Twilight tales
Marjorie Bowen
Oxford City Press, 2011
266 pages
ISBN: 978-1-84902-453-2

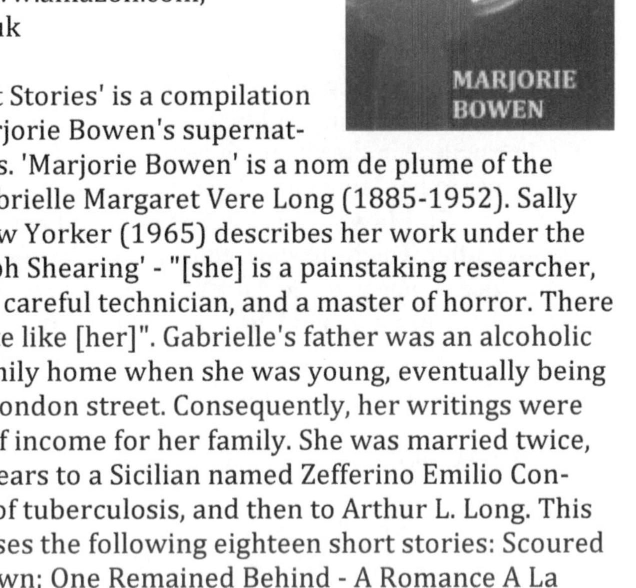

Available from www.amazon.com, www.amazon.co.uk

Collected Twilight Stories' is a compilation of eighteen of Marjorie Bowen's supernatural horror stories. 'Marjorie Bowen' is a nom de plume of the British Author Gabrielle Margaret Vere Long (1885-1952). Sally Benson in The New Yorker (1965) describes her work under the pseudonym 'Joseph Shearing' - "[she] is a painstaking researcher, a superb writer, a careful technician, and a master of horror. There is no one else quite like [her]". Gabrielle's father was an alcoholic and he left the family home when she was young, eventually being found dead on a London street. Consequently, her writings were the main source of income for her family. She was married twice, initially for four years to a Sicilian named Zefferino Emilio Constanza, who died of tuberculosis, and then to Arthur L. Long. This collection comprises the following eighteen short stories: Scoured Silk; The Breakdown; One Remained Behind - A Romance A La Mode Gothique; The House By The Poppy Field; Half-Past Two; Elsie's Lonely Afternoon; The Extraordinary Adventure Of Mr John Proudie; Ann Mellor's Lover; Florence Flannery; Kecksies; The Avenging Of Ann Leete; The Bishop Of Hell; The Crown Derby Plate; The Fair Hair Of Ambrosine; The Housekeeper; Raw Material; The Hidden Ape; The Sign-Painter And The Crystal Fishes

Also from Benediction Books …

Wandering Between Two Worlds: Essays on Faith and Art
Anita Mathias
Benediction Books, 2007
152 pages
ISBN: 0955373700

Available from www.amazon.com, www.amazon.co.uk

In these wide-ranging lyrical essays, Anita Mathias writes, in lush, lovely prose, of her naughty Catholic childhood in Jamshedpur, India; her large, eccentric family in Mangalore, a sea-coast town converted by the Portuguese in the sixteenth century; her rebellion and atheism as a teenager in her Himalayan boarding school, run by German missionary nuns, St. Mary's Convent, Nainital; and her abrupt religious conversion after which she entered Mother Teresa's convent in Calcutta as a novice. Later rich, elegant essays explore the dualities of her life as a writer, mother, and Christian in the United States-- Domesticity and Art, Writing and Prayer, and the experience of being "an alien and stranger" as an immigrant in America, sensing the need for roots.

About the Author

Anita Mathias is the author of *Wandering Between Two Worlds: Essays on Faith and Art*. She has a B.A. and M.A. in English from Somerville College, Oxford University, and an M.A. in Creative Writing from the Ohio State University, USA. Anita won a National Endowment of the Arts fellowship in Creative Nonfiction in 1997. She lives in Oxford, England with her husband, Roy, and her daughters, Zoe and Irene.

Anita's website:
http://www.anitamathias.com, and
Anita's blog Dreaming Beneath the Spires:
http://dreamingbeneaththespires.blogspot.com

The Church That Had Too Much
Anita Mathias
Benediction Books, 2010
52 pages
ISBN: 9781849026567

Available from www.amazon.com, www.amazon.co.uk

The Church That Had Too Much was very well-intentioned. She wanted to love God, she wanted to love people, but she was both hampered by her muchness and the abundance of her possessions, and beset by ambition, power struggles and snobbery. Read about the surprising way The Church That Had Too Much began to resolve her problems in this deceptively simple and enchanting fable.

About the Author

Anita Mathias is the author of *Wandering Between Two Worlds: Essays on Faith and Art*. She has a B.A. and M.A. in English from Somerville College, Oxford University, and an M.A. in Creative Writing from the Ohio State University, USA. Anita won a National Endowment of the Arts fellowship in Creative Nonfiction in 1997. She lives in Oxford, England with her husband, Roy, and her daughters, Zoe and Irene.

Anita's website:
    http://www.anitamathias.com, and
Anita's blog Dreaming Beneath the Spires:
    http://dreamingbeneaththespires.blogspot.com

www.ingramcontent.com/pod-product-compliance
Lightning Source LLC
Chambersburg PA
CBHW021619030826
48979CB00033B/179

* 9 7 8 1 7 8 1 3 9 1 9 0 7 *